HYMN OF MEMORY

HYMN *OF* MEMORY

S. JEAN

Hymn of Memory
Copyright © 2023 by S. Jean
Star*Cadets

Print (paperback) 979-8-987785911
Ebook 979-8-987785904
LCCN: 2023902854

First Edition, 2023, Detroit, MI
Cover art & design by S. Jean

For everyone who believed
in me even when I didn't.

AUTHOR'S NOTE

While *Hymn of Memory* is ultimately about reclaiming a life you once thought forgotten, sometimes you have to hit rock bottom before you climb up to do so. As such, this book contains references to suicide and suicide ideation in addition to themes revolving around grief and death. Please take care when reading!

I.
Memories of Fire

Morgan drew his fingers softly across the death shroud covering the deceased and sparks of memories ignited against his touch. There were more bodies in Rosenburg's morgue than he'd initially thought. Many of them weren't whole; rather, mounds of what once was a person beneath the cloth, the extent of the damage hidden from view. Thankfully, the room didn't smell like death; someone had burned incense to mask it and instead, the tart aroma of cedarwood and rose covered everything.

He'd seen the fire all the way from his spire in Blackburn's priory and while Rosenburg was always alight in the night, twinkling in the distance, the fire had burned brighter. Morgan remembered with vivid clarity how the golden embers rose into the sky and joined the stars before finally fizzling out. He'd been fascinated. At least, until the city got it under control. Then it was a cloud of smoke darkening the sky.

Normally, he wouldn't have made the trek to Rosenburg. His sole purpose was with Blackburn, the town built around his priory, but the city's own Divine, Marcella, was in solitude for another few days and solitude was *never* broken.

So, here Morgan was.

Marcella had come to Blackburn many times when he'd first become Divine five years ago; she'd demonstrated how sendings were done and offered him her vast patience when he'd cried during the process. He supposed he owed her.

The two coroners were giving his clergy escorts—Morgan didn't remember their names; who volunteered switched so often, he'd stopped trying—the details of the dead. Who they'd been, their history, and if they'd left any family behind. Morgan tuned the words out. What mattered right now was their memories.

And the soul contained therein.

Memories clung to the remains, trapping the soul in the carnal flesh. Trapped for too long and the soul would break and truly die, leaving a void.

Divines were meant to help rend the soul free to guide it through the veil and into the Lord of Night's graces for its eventual rebirth. Without Divines, the whole process of rebirth ceased and Morgan didn't like to consider the ramifications.

The whole process felt truer when Morgan could physically touch the skin. It was intimate and real that way, but the head coroner immediately warned him against pulling the shroud back when he reached to do so. She probably worried about the grisly sight and didn't want to frighten Morgan. He was young, after all; much younger than Divines should have been.

He'd deal with the shroud.

Splaying his hands gently against the remains to steady himself, he leaned close to the dead. The cloth veil covering his mouth—a barrier to protect him according to scripture—fell against the remains and he paused. This close, the smell of charred flesh overpowered the incense and made him want to recoil, but he'd smelled worse; he'd deal with it like all Divines did.

Gathering a deep breath, he pressed his lips against the veil and shroud. He exhaled as evenly as he could, letting his breath rustle his veil, and closed his eyes. An invitation to the memories within. They never took long to respond; their body had ceased to answer them and the memories simply saw him as an extension of their own selves and rushed to be heard.

The memories caressed his face, traced his eyes, and whispered to him until he saw a life not his own. Always fleeting. Always fragmented. Someone was loved here; someone was scared there. Snapshots remaining after death, some only surface deep. Memories that must have meant *something* to the deceased, even if Morgan would never understand it on a superficial level.

The fire came as a roaring blaze. Stark and real, it licked across his skin like it danced. The panic surged next; the knowledge of no escape. The world blurred and fuzzed as smoke choked his lungs. Morgan's chest tightened, his eyes watered, and he forced himself to keep breathing. He was not in the fire; there was no smoke coiling in his lungs. He was simply an observer. He gently told the memory it was done, it was over, and the memory stuttered. The fire grew cold and distant until it was nothing more than a flicker in the dark. And the memory released him.

Even the soul had realized it: they'd died.

Morgan straightened his spine, pulling the soul from the remains with deft fingers as though it was a trail of thread. It glittered as it gathered in his hands, becoming a pool of liquid, and like always, it hummed a primordial hymn no one could capture although clergy always tried. Only Divines could see souls like this; they were gifted golden eyes from the Lord of Night along with his celestial touch. To anyone watching, Morgan would be holding and staring at nothing. If they ever looked, at any rate; Morgan learned very quickly no one liked watching the process. Even now, the coroners and his escorts had turned away.

To be fair, they weren't even supposed to be in the room. Priories had private chambers for a Divine's sending, but the bodies had been too fragile to move from the morgue. At the very least, the head coroner had *tried* to make the room as unobtrusive as possible.

Sure, it was still frigid, the steel mortuary drawers on one side reflected the too bright lights, there were large industrial sinks against the far wall not yet cleaned out, and the bodies had been placed on autopsy tables and gurneys in lieu of the typical wooden plinth. The whole room was crowded, but carefully spaced apart to give Morgan room as he moved, robes dragging behind him. The morgue certainly worked on such short notice, but he missed his sending room at his priory.

Sending rooms were antiquated compared to

the morgue; small and mostly wood with gold sconces for candles (his priory had begun to use little electric candles to help prevent any accidents), and his had starry curtains drawn across the walls to mimic a night sky. In the back of the room was a large stained-glass artwork of the Lord of Night, likely to remind Divines he was watching and waiting. Whether that was true or not, at least there Morgan didn't feel out of time as well as out of place.

Thankfully, everyone here had the foresight to turn away and stay quiet, mimicking the hushed silence Morgan was used to during sendings.

The soul nestled in his hands started to slip as Morgan's attention waned and he focused on it again, cupping his hands tighter. The melody it sang had grown quiet and slow, but the glow still pulsed like a heartbeat. Even it went slower the longer Morgan waited. It meant the soul was as ready as it ever would be to pass on. Morgan pressed it to his lips and breathed it in through his veil.

Divine bodies were holy, the mouth most of all. According to scripture, it was through the mouth the souls could pass through the metaphysical veil between worlds. He'd never questioned the process; it seemed to work, even if it was a little cannibalistic. He had sharp teeth for the same reason, but he'd never had to physically rend flesh apart to free souls.

Maybe his precursors had, but thankfully, it had fallen out of fashion.

Like all freed souls who acknowledged their deaths, this one went willingly. It passed through like a cold breath and dissolved down his throat. His vision swam with the sensation, colors glinting to life of the world unseen around them, and hands not his own reached inside, sending a shivering jolt through Morgan's entire body.

Take this soul, Morgan prayed, lips silently mouthing the words behind his veil, *and welcome them into your halls to be reborn.*

The presence took the soul and retreated, leaving fragments of memories the soul had held onto in its wake, and Morgan regained his composure. The Lord of Night—the Lord of the Dead, the one who saw the night chase away the day—was always prompt. Like he was as all-seeing and all-knowing as the texts depicted. Divines knew him intimately, or at least they were said to. If hands plucking the soul out of their throats was intimate.

Once his breathing had evened—once he felt some modicum of normal—Morgan let his gaze float over the rest of the gurneys in the room.

One down, at least half a dozen more to go.

Memories came and went, but some lingered, softly settling within him as they made room for themselves among his own. People he'd never known, people he'd loved and couldn't discern why in the fleeting glimpse, even those he'd hated for a reason he wasn't privy to. Every touch and breath invited the same until it became an exhaustive swirl of memories. Where one ended, another began, and the circle continued on and on.

No matter how gentle everything was, it wore on his body. By the last set of remains, Morgan's knees wobbled, the bile in his stomach churned, and he couldn't lift his hands without trembling. A blinding headache threatened to bloom at the back of his head—not helped at all by the fluorescent electric lights—but deep breaths kept it mostly at bay.

Some Divines dealt with more dead at a time. Dealt with souls who simply refused to believe they were dead, and Morgan could hardly handle a single room.

He hated it.

When he finished, the moment of silent introspection was over. The morgue filled with the head coroner's chatter as she detailed everything she knew about the deceased, the remains, the family, the fire—anything even remotely relevant to the priory's logs. Thankfully, the assisting coroner rescued Morgan from having to feign interest and let him back into the adjoining office to rest in the cushioned rolling chair while his escorts dutifully transcribed everything relevant.

His escorts were regular clergypersons of the priory. Morgan should have had actual attendants who were trained specifically to help him, but none of the recent ones had quite fit. Not that Morgan could remember who'd they'd been. So, this time, these two had volunteered as interim attendants, but in reality, they were merely escorts. Most of the clergy operated in the shadow of the Divine; it showed in what they wore. While the Divine's vestments consisted of a white robe with a gold trim, a black sash and red cord keeping it together in the middle, the clergy's were entirely black. Shadows, literally. Once, they had worn shrouds to mask their entire face, but that had fallen out of fashion because it plainly got in the way.

"I'm sorry," the head coroner said haltingly, drawing Morgan's attention. Though not addressed to him, his curiosity was piqued enough to lean back to peer into the room. "I know it's customary for the bodies to be brought to the priory for this... but..."

The older of his escorts smiled sadly, his eyes crinkling behind his black-rimmed glasses. "Given the circumstances," he said as his partner finished her notes with a flourish, "the trip wasn't uncalled for. Marcella is in solitude and Blackburn isn't truly a long drive. Besides..." He cast a sad glance over the shrouds and Morgan resumed looking away. "They were extremely fragile."

As they continued filling the silence with more inconsequential noise, something to chase away the death in the air no one wanted to confront, Morgan caught the glint of instruments on the desk. Some of them hadn't been cleaned yet and stained a steel tray. He and his entourage had arrived shortly after the city had finished harvesting what organs they could, so they must have just placed it where it would have been out of the way.

Among the instruments was a clean scalpel off to the side. The blade gleamed beneath the light and Morgan couldn't take his gaze away. He ran his fingers delicately across the handle, careful to keep his sleeve from touching anything else. No one said anything or noticed. His pulse sped, a decision made, and he quickly slid the instrument into his sleeve. He'd sewn a pocket inside long before, just to carry something of his, but he hadn't used it yet. And now it was filled.

Just as he retracted his arm, the assisting coroner was beside him with a glass of water. Morgan startled, drawing himself tighter, but all the man did was set the cup down for him.

Like the head coroner, he was older, but Morgan

couldn't discern exactly how old. Skin a healthy tan, not many wrinkles in sight yet, and his hair was a vibrant brown with a dusting of gray within. His lips quirked into a tired smile as he made eye contact and Morgan quickly glanced away. Most weren't ballsy enough to look at the Divine directly. They were scared of death and he *was* death; no one wanted to face their mortality so brazenly.

The assistant looked away soon enough and balked at the tray of instruments. He quickly moved them away from Morgan's line of sight and cleared his throat. "I used to live up in Blackburn, you know."

Morgan brought the cup under his veil and sipped. The water shivered its way down his throat, casting goosebumps across his arms. Despite the sensation, the heat of the flames lingered, searing into his skin as a phantom touch. Nothing real or alarming, just vestiges of memories.

"Ah, where are my manners? My name is Charles," the assistant continued, mistaking Morgan's silence for a reason to keep talking. "My son still lives there, you know. The small town does better for him than here ever did."

Compared to Rosenburg, Blackburn was hardly a town. More of a village. The priory was the oldest building there, up on a hill in the woods. The town had been built around it a long time ago to serve the needs of the Divine and the clergy therein. Since then, the town had grown, becoming something of its own. Though modernization was slow compared to Rosenburg, Blackburn stayed connected to the outside world. Many of the residents frequently traveled to Rosenburg for school, work, and whatever else the city had that they didn't.

"I met Divine Lilia briefly," Charles continued, his voice soft, but still breaking Morgan out of his thoughts again. "She was about my age now when she first became Divine. Well, maybe a year or so younger..." He trailed off and his sudden silence stuck out; he didn't want to say what he'd intended to. At least, not right to Morgan's face.

Morgan was too young to be Divine. Barely even seventeen and already had five years of dealing with dead souls and memories. Everyone *knew* he was too young, but the Lord of Night's decision was absolute. Morgan's hair went white the moment the previous Divine died, denoting him as her successor. Unfortunately, his age meant Morgan hadn't been able to make his own memories—*live*—so he could understand the lives and nuances accompanying the memories before he welcomed them into death. The clergy expected Morgan to simply make it work and he supposed he did. Somehow.

Charles continued rambling after the poignant

pause and spoke about his son instead. He'd be about Morgan's age. What was left unsaid, of course, was if Morgan had been normal, they would have gone to school together. Maybe even been friends. All Morgan did was nod and sip his water. Charles didn't need a reply; he just wanted to talk away the guilt he felt putting Morgan through this. Like it was his fault. It wasn't.

The fault was the Lord of Night's alone.

Silence was a relief when the head coroner called Charles back into the room to finish moving the bodies into the mortuary drawers. By then, Morgan's escorts had come in and they left together with little fanfare. The city around them was winding down for the night, but it would never truly be silent like the morgue had been. Cars of all kinds rumbled their way down the street, engines loud along the evening breeze, and there was the distant chatter of a crowd a few streets over. The noise was a stark contrast to the silence of the dead.

Life simply moved on from the devastating fire that claimed the poor souls caught within. Soon, after vigils and mourning, the fire itself would become a hazy memory, forgotten as the days wore on. Lost to the noise of the day-to-day. Only Morgan would remember it with vivid clarity.

The cab Rosenburg had loaned them still waited

on the street in front of the morgue and as soon as they emerged, its engine joined the chorus of the vehicles around them. All Morgan wanted was silence, but he refrained from complaining and climbed into the back to begin the drive home. Blackburn Priory had no vehicles of its own; it had no space for them. Although, it wasn't like Blackburn *needed* its own cabs; the town was too small. If Morgan needed to be brought into town for any reason, he wouldn't mind walking. As it was, most things needing his attention came to the priory for him. Rosenburg never minded loaning one of their cabs and a driver, at least, should the need arise.

The cab wasn't wholly uncomfortable, just a little old. The driver was separated from them by a screen between the front and backseats and this driver didn't make much small talk. The back was fitted like an old carriage with two sets of cushioned seats facing one another. The clergy put their backs to the driver while Morgan settled in on the opposite side. He wasn't keen on being squished between them like they'd been on the drive there.

Darkened city buildings slid by, but nothing interesting stood out from the brief glance Morgan afforded them as they drove. It was only when they left the city limits did the buildings finally thin and Morgan lifted his gaze.

Evening had stolen the blue out of the sky and the color melted into something like fire along the horizon. Even the gleam of the sun cut through the cab's front windows, burning into Morgan's eyes. The smell of concrete and gasoline finally gave way to the aroma of late summer as the air whistled through the opening in the window. The breeze cooled Morgan's face and he breathed in deep, welcoming the oncoming autumn air as it filled his lungs. It wouldn't be long before the leaves themselves transformed into their own medley of fire.

Flames licked his arms, coating them, and he set his jaw, holding himself tighter. No. It was just a memory wanting to be remembered. He gently eased himself against the back of the seat, reminding himself the fire was not real—not to him anyway— and searched for a distraction beyond the hum of the cab.

His escorts spoke amongst themselves with soft murmurs of the day-to-day. They never made conversation with him. Hardly anyone did. If someone chanced it, it was like the coroner's assistant: rambling to mask nervousness stemming from being so close to Morgan. It came with being Divine. Too holy to relate to. Too holy to think they were owed a real conversation. Morgan had simply become used to it. He wouldn't even know what to say if someone actually tried engaging him in a genuine conversation.

They wouldn't help. They never did.

Perhaps listening had been distraction enough however; his robes were free of flickering flames and he relaxed.

He caught his reflection in the window and frowned at how tired he appeared. Today was almost over, at least. Soon he'd return to the priory halls he knew so well. He closed his eyes and rested his head against the window, glad the glass was cool.

My name is Morgan, he told himself and silently moved his lips beneath his veil, feeling the cloth brush against his lips. *My mother's name is Cynthia. My father's name is Joseph.* He breathed out, his pulse quickening. Those were their names. They had to be. *My name is Morgan*, he repeated, focusing deeper to get it right. *My mother's name is Cynthia. My father's name is Charles.* He bit his lip, lancing pain through it from his sharp teeth, and released it just as fast.

No. His father's name was not Charles. It was Joseph. Memories muddied, fast and quick like they were taunting him with what was real and what was simply someone else's memory that had fashioned itself a place in Morgan's thoughts.

My name is Morgan, he began again, gritting his teeth. *My mother was a baker. She hummed to me when I was little. Her name is...* His thoughts came up blank. Empty. His pulse pounded in his ears. He'd already lost what they'd looked like. Whenever he thought of them now, they were blank faces with features too fuzzy to discern. He couldn't even remember if he'd had siblings. He'd been told family would have been a distraction from his duties and maybe they'd been encouraged to leave Blackburn. Many times, when he was younger, he'd eyed those in attendance at sermons searching for them, but he'd never find them. Now, he had no idea what they looked like. Sounded like. Both were forgone memories in a sea of those not his own.

It didn't really matter, Morgan supposed. Without recognizing them, he wouldn't know where to start with searching for them. Besides, if they cared, wouldn't they have tried to talk to him by now?

Yet still, he held onto their names because it was all he had. Their details wouldn't come. Nor would the corrections. All that came to him were the memories drowned out by fire. People he'd never met. Lives he'd already sent through the veil waiting for one last chance to be real to someone. The images lingered, overcoming his own like always.

Every single day, something slipped away from him, stripping him from being Morgan.

"Your Holiness?" the younger clergy asked, her

voice sweet and melodic. She and her partner had ceased speaking. Morgan wasn't sure how long ago. She furrowed her eyebrows in worry. "Are you all right?"

"The fire was a lot," the other said, even as Morgan opened his mouth to answer for himself. "I can send for some milk tea to help soften the images when we return."

"No," Morgan said, his own voice foreign to him. "No. I'm only tired. That's all."

His escorts watched him a moment before they shared a quick glance. A silent conversation with a single look. They pitied him, even if they'd do nothing about it but suggest he forget it. The priory's milk tea wouldn't help; Morgan had no idea what it was made of, except it was a milky texture with a taste too subtle to pin down. Every time he drank it, the world became too fuzzy and distant, making memories painfully hard to reach.

It never helped.

"I'll send some up anyway," the older escort said softly. "You can drink it, or you can leave it."

The younger one nodded. "For now, sleep! It's a long ride."

It always was.

Morgan rested against the window again, letting the ghost of summer rustle through his hair, and closed his eyes. He wouldn't sleep; if he did, memories would resurface as dreams, molding him into someone he never was. Instead of succumbing, he repeated his mantra to himself again. Searching deep for the names which had long since escaped.

My name is Morgan.

One day, Morgan feared when he awoke, he wouldn't even remember his own name and no one would care.

II.

THE HEAD PRIOR

The moon had ascended high in the sky by the time they entered Blackburn. Everything was shuttered until the morning with few homes still illuminated with lamps or flickering televisions. The streetlights led the cab through the empty streets and up the dark path to the priory on the hill in the woods. The priory was mostly dark as well with only electric candles left lit in the windows as invitation for any weary traveler (not that such a thing was common nowadays). Although to Morgan, it made the whole building look more haunting than inviting.

Though the priory had dormitories for dedicated clergy, the days they were used had come and gone. The clergy now commuted to and from

Blackburn and the only time the dormitories were used was when out of town clergy visited. Of Blackburn's staff, there was a handful during the day of which Morgan's escorts were part of and then the night crew made up of mostly housekeepers. While Morgan's days were filled with contemplation and his Divine duties, he wasn't quite sure what the clergy filled their time with when there wasn't a pressing matter. He'd never had reason to ask.

As it was, only Morgan and the Head Prior had permanent lodgings in the priory itself. Morgan's was at the top of the priory's spire like all other Divines before him; it kept the Divine separated and sacred. The Head Prior, meanwhile, had his space in the empty dormitory alongside anyone that may have been visiting. It kept him near and available.

Wherever he slept, the priory was home and home meant sleep.

Until Morgan stepped inside with his attendants and the night clergy on duty let them know the Head Prior wanted to speak to them upon their return.

The Head Prior's office was above the chapel room used for morning and evening services. It allowed him to always be near the main room of worship just in case.

The entire place was dimmed for the night except for his office. It was a blaze in the dark, burning into Morgan's eyes as he followed his escorts inside and took another moment for his vision to readjust.

Morgan hadn't been in the Head Prior's office too often; if the prior wanted to speak to him, he generally came to Morgan's room instead. Morgan disliked his office. It was too clean, too neat, and always felt as though he was putting on a front for anyone who came in. The lights suspended from the ceiling hummed with electricity, boring into Morgan's skull as his earlier headache from the sending crawled back, and he quickly focused on anything else to keep it at bay.

The prior's wooden desk took up much of the room and upon it was another lit lamp, illuminating the scrolls from past sendings Morgan had done earlier in the year. With them was an old telephone, a rotary card file, and a typewriter. Flanking the opened window behind the desk were bookcases, each one perfectly arranged with histories, scriptures, and whatever else the Head Prior thought important enough to display. Everything was neat, had its place, and made Morgan feel out of place himself.

The Head Prior sat at his desk and despite how late it was—maybe he'd stayed in his office all evening waiting for their return—he was still dressed in his clergy finery; black like all the others, but his had been decorated with golden fastenings that practically gleamed underneath the light, setting him apart.

As soon as they were settled in, Morgan's escorts began speaking. They told the Head Prior what the coroner had said and rattled off what they had written in their notes. Like before, Morgan tuned them out; all of it would be there for him tomorrow and right now, sleep beckoned. Instead of nodding off right then and there and earning the Head Prior's disdain, he searched for another distraction.

He slipped his hands into his sleeves and his thumb brushed the handle of the scalpel hidden away. For some reason, he hadn't expected it to still be there. And even more, no one knew he had it. The thought alone made his pulse quicken, especially when *why* he'd wanted it crossed his mind. No. He left it alone and placed his hands back in his lap.

My name is Morgan, he mouthed to himself in lieu of anything else. *My mother's name is—*

"I'd like to speak to His Holiness alone, actually," the Head Prior interrupted Morgan's mantra and he jerked his attention back to the room. His escorts stared at the prior, as confused as he was, and the air between them weighed heavy.

A private audience so late, especially one after a sending as grisly as the one Morgan had endured was odd. Keeping the Divine away from rest was odder still.

The older escort recovered first, readjusting his glasses. "He needs rest," he said slowly, like he was testing the waters of insubordination. His partner cast her eyes downward and collected her notes from the desk. He was on his own. "It has been a *very* long day."

"I don't intend to keep him long," the Head Prior said, raising his eyebrows. "You can wait outside and once we're finished, you can take him to his room and tuck him in."

Even though Morgan desperately wished they'd stay, it wasn't like they could. The Head Prior's word was absolute and if he wanted to talk to Morgan, well, he would. Everyone always said he had the Divine's best interests at heart, though Morgan wondered if the sentiment was true. He was sure the Head Prior actually disliked him for the simple fact Morgan had the audacity to be a child when he was made Divine, making the Head Prior's job harder.

Not like Morgan had a say in that.

His escorts made their leave without any further protest and as the door closed, Morgan studied the Head Prior. He hardly ever saw the man as it was and now that he was fully awake, starkly in reality instead of the fuzzy half-dream threatening to pull him under from how exhausted he was, he figured he should at least *try* to commit some of the man to memory.

The Head Prior had the position when Morgan became Divine and given his age, perhaps he'd had it since the beginning of the previous Divine. He was middle-aged with pale skin age had pulled taut. His eyes were a dark brown, never anything that invited warmth and his hair was just as dark, nary a gray strand in sight, but it had begun to recede. Curiously, his eyebrows were a pale blond; perhaps he dyed his hair because it had turned lighter with age, making it more white than blond. White hair was strictly for Divines, but most people could tell when it was the white locks of divinity versus hair simply gone white with age. Perhaps it was simply vanity so he didn't appear as old, although Morgan wasn't sure why he even bothered—

"Your Holiness?" the Head Prior's voice crashed through Morgan's thoughts once more, pulling him back, and he tilted his head as Morgan met his gaze. He must have said something that warranted an answer.

Morgan swallowed. "Yes?" he said, his voice still weaker than he wanted.

There was a slow inhale, but the man didn't outright sigh. Morgan was sure if he'd been anyone else, the Head Prior would have already announced his annoyance. Being the Divine had its perks for once. The Head Prior instead brought his hands together on the desk and laced his fingers together. "I was asking you: what did the memories show you?"

"Fire. Lots of it." Morgan frowned behind his veil and the Head Prior hesitated, like he'd been expecting something more. Growing uneasy under the man's stare, Morgan shifted in his chair. His pulse raced thinking of what he could have missed. Nothing. It was just lives consumed by fire. He cleared his throat. "W-What is it you want, Prior...?"

Though Morgan intended otherwise, he'd ended with a pause, searching for the name he'd long since lost to the haze of memories. He shut his mouth, hoping it wasn't noticed.

"Augustus," the Head Prior said.

"P-Pardon?"

"That's my name. *Augustus*." He enunciated the syllables slowly, as if it would help. Morgan gently bit down on his lip, trying to hide his annoyance. "Come now. We've been through this numerous times."

Too many times to count. Scant memories of conversations and being reminded of his name in the same fake, playful tone. It grew increasingly withered and annoyed each time because Morgan couldn't remember something so simple. It probably hurt his pride. Not like it mattered; Morgan didn't *want* to remember. Their lives hardly intersected in any meaningful way as it was. Remembering his name meant another name Morgan wanted to keep might slip away.

Besides, it wasn't like anyone had ever said Morgan's name. They probably didn't even remember it. All he was to them was the Divine.

Nothing more.

Still, Morgan sighed, releasing his agitation with the breath, and nodded. "Prior *Augustus*," he repeated quietly. "I am *very* tired. What is it you need from me?"

Prior Augustus leaned back, studying Morgan with narrowed eyes. Morgan quickly looked at anything else. From the clock ticking in time with Morgan's heartbeat, to the priory heraldry hanging from the ceiling against the wall to the side, and then to the open window behind Prior Augustus.

"All I want are the details."

"And you will have them when I write them." Annoyance leaked into Morgan's voice despite his best efforts. After every sending, one of the duties of the Divine was to transcribe the memories still lingering after the Lord of Night took the deceased's soul. It was said to help the Divine let go of memories that weren't theirs. It didn't always work. When

Morgan finished, he handed it off to the clergy scribes who would transcribe a copy for the families and the original would be locked in the priory vaults as a record of who lived and passed in Blackburn. The ones from the fire would be shipped to Rosenburg when they were finished.

"Forcing the memories won't do any good," Morgan continued. "All I see right now is fire and all I feel is terror. Nothing else."

Prior Augustus paused, jaw clenched. A tinge of annoyance he could hardly hide. "Yes," he said, dragging out the word. "Beyond the terror, however, did any of those you sent feel... guilt about the fire itself?"

Morgan straightened and stared directly at Prior Augustus. He finally realized *what* the man was trying to do: figure out if it was arson. Theoretically, a trained and seasoned Divine could sift through lingering memories in such a way to find motive and intent. Why he expected Morgan to be able to do it, however, left Morgan confused.

"I was told," Prior Augustus continued, keeping eye contact, "the building was a small café. They all should have been able to get out."

There was pounding on locked doors. For some reason, they wouldn't open. The sound reverberated through Morgan, stark and real like Prior Augustus' own door was rattling from fists. His lungs seized, struggling to draw in air as he smelled smoke. His throat was raw from screaming and no one answered but more screams. The inferno had grown too fast, igniting all the wood inside faster than it should have if it *had* been an accident.

"All I wanted to do," Prior Augustus' voice was the bridge back and Morgan focused on it. Not the way the room was sparking around him. Not the screams inviting themselves into his mind because they wanted to be remembered. "Was to be of help to the Rosenburg detectives who are sure to come down anon expecting answers." The room was still warm, even without the flames. "If you could just tell me *who* set the fire—*who* locked the doors..."

All Prior Augustus wanted was the glory. Even Morgan could plainly see that. Solve it before the Rosenburg detectives could. It would prove to *someone* the Blackburn Priory had a Divine worth a damn. Marcella might have been able to do it; she knew her divinity inside and out and had perfect guile and poise every time Morgan had seen her. Not like him. If only she hadn't been in solitude. If only she had been there to see to the bodies herself.

The room had grown so much warmer. Fire licked around his chair, but he dared not stare at it directly. Doing so would only show Prior Augustus he was unraveling. The chair turned to ash beneath the flames, but somehow, he and the cushion stayed perilously afloat, even as the fires danced across his sleeves next. The wooden floorboards took the flames farther until they caught the priory heraldry. It went aflame, growing bright and golden behind Prior Augustus.

Flames that weren't real. Not here. Never here.

"No," Morgan said and Prior Augustus' jaw tightened again, but his face remained impassive. "I do not believe I feel anything you are insinuating." Morgan twisted his hands together, trying not to watch the fire as it traced itself across the ceiling beam above them. "Nor am I willing to entertain any more thoughts on the matter because it would only color my perception of their memories."

They stared at one another for far too long in silence. Morgan wasn't well-versed in telling anyone no, especially not Prior Augustus; in fact, he was sure *no one* told Prior Augustus no and the man simply wasn't used to it. Denying what he wanted, however, let the silence linger for too long in the creeping heat and twinkling embers fell from the ceiling beams ablaze above them.

Finally, Prior Augustus sighed and a breeze from the window followed it. Cool, it brought with it the smells of the forest around the priory, and all the flames ceased. Reality slotted back into place, returning everything to what it once was.

Whole.

"Could I retire to my room, now?" Morgan asked, a tremble in his voice.

"You may," Prior Augustus said. "Just remember what I've said. We can stop this from happening again."

"If they're already dead," Morgan said slowly, "will it matter?"

Prior Augustus was forgetting the plain reality and truth right in front of them. While he wanted to be important, what mattered was those who died inside the flames. Never to live again. They deserved peace. Not to have their memories unearthed again and again to relive their final moments for some clue that was never there to begin with.

"Yes." Prior Augustus once more dragged out the word. "I see what a toll this has been on you and I apologize for keeping you." He wasn't. "I think a week of solitude is in order. You haven't needed one in a while, but given how many memories you have to sift through, I think it is appropriate."

A whole week. Morgan paused, his stomach twisting. "T-The—" He stopped and swallowed as Prior Augustus raised his eyebrows. "The Autumnal Equinox Service is coming up in a few days."

"I'm aware." Augustus slowly nodded. "You've

never liked attending the services before, however. Did you change your mind?"

The equinox and solstice services were serious affairs to pay reverence to the passage of time and the shifting of the seasons. They'd remember those who passed away, officially welcome those who were born, and give people time to examine their lives with others. Blackburn was small enough they only performed one service in the evening, but a city like Rosenburg had at least two—one in the morning and evening. As Divine—the Lord of Night's conduit—he was supposed to attend them because it was said the veil was thin on those days and allowed the Lord of Night and Lady of Dawn to truly listen to the world.

Prior Augustus was not wrong; Morgan disliked the services. The number of people made him nervous, especially because many of those attending would want to talk to Morgan after the sermon was finished. Anyone who spoke to him was kind, at the very least—all they wanted was a connection to their Divine—but Morgan had no idea what to say to them. He simply felt like he was playing dress-up instead of being a real Divine like Marcella who had her own sermons and spoke to her people with ease. All he did during services was sit there, listening, and occasionally helped the Head Prior light candles if it was warranted.

Nothing he truly needed to be there for.

Morgan shook his head. "I-If you do not need me for it, then a week of solitude is fine," he said quietly. "Thank you."

Prior Augustus saw him out of the office and to his two escorts still waiting. They exchanged words about the forthcoming solitude, but Morgan didn't listen too intently. All he wanted, desperately, was to sleep.

His escorts finally took him into the spire for his room and each step upward was real, a reminder he was still awake and not in some fuzzy dream. When they reached the top, it wasn't much longer before he was out of his Divine vestments and into his nightclothes. Wasn't long before he washed up and emerged, keeping his veil on only because his escorts had taken it upon themselves to ready his bed even when they didn't have to.

The bed took up the most space in his small room. A large cream-colored canopy covered it, normally kept pinned against the bedposts. The sheer fabric allowed him to remain unveiled in his own room if someone needed to come in for whatever reason. It made the world beyond fuzzy and soft. In the morning, the sun always hit it just right and allowed light to shimmer as it came through. Sometimes, all Morgan wanted to do was watch as the sunlight gleamed through the fabric.

Morgan shook himself out of his thoughts. Morning would come and so would the fuzzy sunlight. For now, sleep.

As he opened his mouth to thank them, he noticed the teacup placed on the nightstand beside the bed. He frowned, narrowing his eyes.

"I said I didn't need it."

"I know," the older clergy replied. "But just in case you change your mind."

Morgan bit down; it wasn't worth the repeated argument. Especially with how fast they'd brought it up. Between the fire and talking to the Head Prior, they probably assumed he'd need *something*. Leaving it was born out of their guilt for forcing him through this. Something to absolve them of their said guilt. Their way of apologizing for everything.

Whatever their intent, he'd let it grow cold and dump it out in the morning. The tea never worked the way they wanted anyway. What was meant to help dull the severity of memories invited inside—keep them from feeling real—simply left Morgan's thoughts fuzzy and numb. A quiet panic attack he couldn't escape from until it ran its course. Not helpful. He released a slow breath and left it be.

"Thank you," Morgan whispered.

His escorts wished him a good night and filed

out, shutting the door behind them.

Alone. He finally unclasped his veil, breathing in deep, and set it in the wardrobe with the rest of his vestments. The clergy had already carefully hung his robe and taken his other clothes to have them cleaned. He closed the wardrobe and shut away his divinity.

"My name is Morgan," he told himself, verbalizing it and felt the way his lips moved to say his own name aloud when no one else would.

Still his name. He wouldn't let himself forget, even if no one spoke it. Even if he forgot everyone else's.

With another breath, sleep etching at the corner of his vision, he faced his bed.

In the summer, it was dressed in thin blankets, while in the winter he had at least three or more keeping him warm. The only constant was the colorful knitted blanket his father had sent with him when he became Divine. Though he wasn't sure if his father had knitted it himself or if it was some family heirloom, he was glad he had it. Something wholly his.

The clergy had made sure to pull it out and lay it above the others for Morgan. Kindness among the silence. Even in the dark, he could trace the colors if he wanted to, each variegated thread as it morphed from one color to the next. It soothed him. He breathed out and let himself fall into all the colors.

And he kept falling through and into the dark where fires sparked in the distance at the edge of a dream.

III.

SOLITUDE

⁓⁓⁓

Solitude wasn't anything new; Divines were typically granted it after difficult sendings. It was to digest what they'd seen without distraction and allow them to come to terms with it. Death came for everyone, but it wasn't always pretty. Images remained—as Morgan starkly recalled as he awoke—regret persisted, and if not dealt with, would become part of the Divine, like it was their own memory to begin with.

In that way, solitude was a blessing and a curse.

As a blessing, Morgan was away from duties requiring him elsewhere in the priory. He didn't have to attend Holy Day Mass and was completely relieved from having to train his expression to one of soft reflection instead of how tired he really was.

It let him be Morgan in a sea of memories threatening to undo him instead of someone playing dress-up as Divine.

On the curse side, however, he was truly alone with memories that ceased to be his long ago.

At noon, after he was given lean non-perishable meals to last the week, his door was shut with a red cord pulled around the handle, front and back. It would not break until his solitude was completed and it made sure no one would disturb him. It was mostly symbolic; to take it off, all Morgan had to do was untie his side and it would release the other. He was never trapped per se, but it still felt like he was.

The first thing Morgan did was leave his robe and veil in the wardrobe. The lack of both made him feel more like himself. The clothes worn underneath the robe were thin and snug, perfect for warmer days. They consisted of a fitted sleeveless black tunic that buttoned up the side and it had a matching set of black leggings. He kept the red cord from the Divine ensemble around his waist, perhaps out of a sense of duty to at least try to appear as devout as previous Divines, but in all honesty, he liked the red pop of color.

With solitude being his alone, he had no reason to pretend otherwise. *Yes*, he decided. He wore it because he liked red and that was that.

His room was different during the day than at night, especially when locked in solitude. With light and not aching for sleep, the room was a stark reminder it had once been a place where all previous Divines throughout Blackburn's history had lived. And yet, despite its history, it lacked any lasting personal touch. Perhaps it was on purpose.

The walls were made of brick and stone while wooden ceiling beams crisscrossed above him, reminding him of the rest of the priory. The room had even been outfitted with electric lights like the rest of the building, although now the bronze fixtures holding the bulbs appeared antiquated compared to what Morgan had seen in Rosenburg's morgue. He preferred leaving the lights off as long as possible. Less buzzing. Sunlight was plenty.

Besides, sunlight had a pretty way of glinting off the clear baubles Morgan had hung from the ceiling (they'd been a gift, although Morgan couldn't remember from whom); when the light caught them, the baubles cast prisms of color across the walls. When he died, they'd be taken down like he hadn't existed at all and the room would become impersonal again.

The single window across from the door overlooked the wooded path down to Blackburn. On clear days, Morgan could see all the way there and to

Rosenburg. The sun always crested the horizon behind Rosenburg's own priory, lighting it up like it really was holy. Once it passed the top, the sun shined through Morgan's window. Nice in the winter when it was frigid, but dreadful in the summer.

At the front of the bed was a wooden chest engraved with wildflowers. It was meant for the personal effects of the Divine, items they would have brought with them when they first arrived. Morgan hardly had anything. At the age of twelve, he hadn't quite understood he wasn't going home. All he had were old clothes he'd quickly outgrown and a photo bleached from leaving it in the sun once, ridding the faces of their details.

Try as he might, the faces never resurfaced in his memory.

Near the bed, beside the door to his personal bathroom, was his wardrobe. All it held was his ceremonial robes—one for summer made with breezy fabric; the other for winter with a fur trim and multiple layers—a wooden sphere to hold his veil, and drawers where garments to wear underneath the robes were folded. Nothing truly his. Once, he'd tried hanging the clothes he'd come with, but a well-meaning clergyperson had stopped him, saying the wardrobe was for the Divine vestments only. Not Morgan's. He was sure she'd meant to be helpful, but her words somehow stuck. Morgan didn't matter; only the Divine did.

Lastly, across from the bed, now plainly seen as sunlight shined through the window, was a wooden desk. Though a far cry from magnificence of the Head Prior's desk, it was quaint and the perfect size for anything Morgan had to do. A hutch fashioned with shelves sat atop it and many sending scrolls stuck out. There were drawers of pens and inkwells, sheaves of paper piled in one corner, and a book of scripture hardly touched now. The chair was stiff, draped in Divine heraldry, and Morgan hated sitting in it. He'd much rather spread his instruments across the bed and work from there, but somehow it didn't feel right when he tried.

For better or worse, the room was all he had for an entire week of solitude.

The first day was... nice. Morgan soaked in the bathroom's tub to forget what the Head Prior had told him. Someone had left him a bottle of rosewater and lavender to mix in to help him relax and he'd liberally poured it in with the usual bubbles. He might have soaked longer than he'd meant to; the water was just so gentle against the dreams of fire that had plagued him all night. The bath washed away the phantom crackle against his skin and soothed away the burning in his lungs when he breathed in deep. Even more, there was the frosted window in the bathroom which had a splash of color. When the sun hit it, colorful shimmers danced across the walls and Morgan got lost watching them turn with the sun.

Eventually, the water grew cold and he convinced himself to move on with his day. He'd covered the mirror in the bathroom long ago and resisted peering into it as he dried off. Every time he did, he hardly recognized himself and he hated to be reminded. No one ever uncovered the mirror when they came to clean, thankfully. Maybe they pitied him for it.

Next, he tried to reflect and pray like he was told to do when he was uneasy. He certainly still was, despite the bath. Scripture stated the Lord of Night welcomed the dead, plied their judgement (although the texts were unclear what exactly he did as judgement), and put them to rest, while the Lady of Dawn, once she felt the souls were ready, replanted them in babes born anew. It forever preserved the cycle of life and death. It should have been soothing knowing life always continued in some form or another.

Being Divine, Morgan figured he'd have inside knowledge, reassurance it *was* the truth, but he didn't. Memories *always* lingered after a sending, even when the soul was gone into the Lord of Night's embrace. If memories were left behind, what else was? Why they lingered at all, however, Morgan could never explain and no scripture he'd found could either. He simply did his job, hoping it was right, and prayed the deceased's family didn't ask for his confidence that scripture was the unshakable truth. He didn't want to lie and say he was sure when he wasn't. No one could be sure but the Lord and Lady.

When prayers and reflection left him frustrated instead of satiated like they were supposed to, he finished the day transcribing memories.

The act was meant to help him let go of the memory, while also preserve something of the life that once was so the priory had recollection of it. The scrolls had already been started with flourished handwriting. There were the names, the day the Lady of Dawn breathed life into them, and the day they breathed their last and the Lord of Night accepted them into his halls.

The names helped most of all. Their memories leapt to the forefront of Morgan's thoughts when he read something wholly theirs. Morgan dipped his pen nib into the archaic inkwell the clergy provided and let the memory guide his hand. Most Divines were said to wear their ceremonial robes during this process, but all Morgan had done when he'd tried was smear ink all over his sleeve. Most Divines apparently weren't left-handed.

The memories guided his hand with ease. Details about the fire, how scared they'd been, but also smaller things. Like what they'd done that morning before their life was taken. Even about their loved ones they wanted to recall one last time. Human touches that made them more than a scream in the dark inferno. Morgan tried not to linger on anything the memories wrote; he wanted no personal connection with the deceased. No Divine truly did; it colored their perceptions of what the memories meant and Morgan wanted to preserve what the memory truly was, not write it through his own perceptions. He owed the dead at least that much.

Especially as the Head Prior's voice weaseled its way back into Morgan's thoughts, making him think of who set the fire. He shut it away and focused deeper on the memories guiding his hand. He owed it to the dead to stay focused—get the memories *right*—and owed the Head Prior nothing.

On the second day of solitude, his hands trembled too much to write. He hadn't slept. The fire had returned and kept him awake; he'd watched it dance across his bed, watched it coat the ceiling beams above the canopy, and watched as the embers rained down on him. The roof caved in soon enough and he'd struggled to breathe as his lungs burned.

It wasn't real. Deep down, he knew that, but closing his eyes to ignore it simply plunged him into another nightmare coated in fire.

What didn't help was the scroll with no name. It had a suggestion of how old they were from the coroner's notes and what they'd had with them when the body was found, but no name. Someone died and no one knew who they were and everyone somehow expected Morgan to filter their memories from the rest. The memory absolutely refused to surface and instead, plunged him over and over into panic as he tried to extract it from his own.

All that responded was the fire. Like it was becoming his own memory instead of one that should never have been his to begin with.

It wasn't supposed to be like this.

Frustration sent his arm across the desk, throwing the scroll to the floor, the inkwell farther. Ink stained the sorry corner it landed in and Morgan raked his hands through his hair.

Divines were supposed to be untouchable, unflappable, completely holy and in control over their divinity. And here he was, struggling with the simplest duty he had. Extracting memory from his own. Remembering the dead.

How could he remember the dead if he could hardly remember himself?

The question undid him entirely and the rest of the day was lost to a nightmare of fire as he curled up tight on his bed, trying to will it away.

The third day, he didn't bother to get out of bed or eat the soup and bread he'd been left with. It wasn't like he disliked it, even if the flavor was plain to keep from distracting him. Just when he thought of rising to eat, he wanted to vomit instead.

Sleep never came no matter how long he stayed in bed. The lack of it pulled his body taut, worming pain throughout every single muscle.

He stared at the canopy atop his bed, his head sunk in his pillows, and a soft summer breeze trickled its way through the room. It was so quiet; all he could do was listen to the racing heart inside his chest. He couldn't calm it down. His breathing became ragged and uneven, like he was truly trying to breathe through smoke even though it wasn't there and he knew it.

Without realizing it, he'd brought the scalpel out. All he'd done was hold it. The weight was too real in his hand, like for some reason it shouldn't have been, and he simply stared at it as the sun glinted off the blade. The fires ceased as he did, the memories hushed as though waiting, and then it was just him and the blade.

Maybe the obtrusive thoughts of escape should have frightened him. Except deep down, they meant escape from himself, from his responsibility, and from everything everyone expected of him. Still, he didn't move to entertain anything filtering through his silent thoughts uninvited.

"What would you think," Morgan whispered to possibly no one, "seeing me in your graces too early?" He swallowed and waited for a response he knew was never coming. The Lord of Night was only ever there during sendings, Morgan was sure of it. He was speaking to no one. His exhale escaped as a shaking breath. "Would you be disappointed? Take pity and send me home so I could just be me again?"

The questions and lack of answers made tears prickle in the corner of his eyes. It didn't matter. If he did go out now, he'd at least be himself. Morgan. What few memories he'd managed to hold onto wholly his. Not the ghost he'd become as Divine.

A sound disrupted all the empty thoughts. He blinked and peered through the shroud covering his bed. There was a step, he was sure of it, on the roof. No one should have been there. It was so high up; how did they get there to begin with? The steps were careful, even, like they'd slip otherwise, and something cracked. Too much weight leaned on a tile desperately needing repair. Another crack answered the first; they'd overcorrected and slammed their foot down, if Morgan had to guess.

This time, debris sprinkled the top of the canopy.

Oh, Morgan thought distantly to himself. *The roof's breaking.* It *was* old; no one had touched it in such a long time. He was surprised it hadn't blown off during the last summer storm.

The thoughts were dull, unsurprised, but when sunlight peeked through the roof and someone cursed, the thoughts repeated themselves with urgency. Morgan's heart jolted.

The roof was breaking above him.

And it did, bringing with it debris and a person.

Morgan thought for sure the ceiling beam would stop most of it. Namely the person. They hit it, definitely—there was a pained grunt and then a yelp when they hadn't managed to hold on—but then continued downward anyway, hitting the canopy with their entire weight and part of the roof with them.

Morgan bit back a scream, teeth piercing his lips, and he couldn't even see what he struggled against when the canopy folded in on itself. The bedposts broke, brittle wood finally giving way, and everything heaped itself upon Morgan. Whoever had come through the roof thrashed, long limbs entangling themselves in the fabric, and they jostled Morgan around as they moved. Morgan shoved the wayward limbs out of his way and fought to get out from underneath everything.

At least the beam hadn't come down too.

Between his heart trying to break out of his chest and the fuzzy feeling overcoming his body from all the panic and adrenaline, he found the edge of his bed. He awkwardly slipped off and thumped on the floor, but at least he was out of the mess, even if his heart was slow to realize it.

He crawled backward until his back hit the wall and the scalpel was in his hands again—this time a weapon to protect himself. How he hadn't lost it in the scuffle, he wasn't sure; it must have been some sense of self-preservation rather than the answer to the obtrusive thoughts.

All the thrashing on the bed ceased, and a very long sigh escaped the folds of fabric as everything settled. A leg extracted itself from the mess first and then a young man followed shortly after. He sunk to the floor, pressing a hand to the back of his head, and he grimaced, glancing around.

The young man blinked, his eyes a very warm shade of brown, and their gazes met. He opened his mouth like he was halfway between saying something or gawking, but no sound came out. All it did was draw Morgan's gaze to the young man's mouth. The soft curve his lips made paired with how sharp his jaw and cheekbones were lit a memory too fuzzy to discern from the others.

He was perhaps Morgan's age, or a little older, and lean beneath his white tank top and black and red hooded jacket. His brown trousers were rolled up from his ankles and he had scuffed white sneakers. A bracelet adorned one wrist as a braided relic of summer's past with bleached colors, a contrast to his light brown skin. Dark freckles danced across his nose and cheeks, making him look younger. His hair, disheveled from the fall, was a rich brown, flung back from his forehead as a short wave, and strands glimmered gold beneath the stream of light from the hole in the roof.

"Uh," the young man finally spoke, although it wasn't something coherent. A jammed word ending up as an awkward sound. He'd gone incredibly still, looking Morgan over like Morgan had done to him. Suddenly, Morgan felt self-conscious and pulled himself tighter. "Hey." The young man cleared his throat. "A-Are you okay? I didn't mean to fall on you."

Morgan snapped his hands to his mouth, dropping the scalpel. The young man's gaze trailed after it, confused, and then right back to Morgan.

"You broke the roof," Morgan said, the first thought to verbalize. He chanced a glance over his shoulder at the door; the cord around the handles remained intact and no voices floated up from the hall about the racket. Did no one hear it?

Morgan eyed the young man again. His expression was hurt, but as soon as he noticed Morgan staring again, his lips shifted into a weak smile.

"Well," he said, "it's not like I meant to."

"No." Morgan's heart was going to break through his chest with how hard it was pounding. "Do you know who I am?"

It was another second before the young man startled. His gaze swung to the half-opened wardrobe beside Morgan and he practically dove at it. Morgan clattered out of the way, heart pounding even faster in his chest, and it only slowed when he realized what the young man was doing.

He was searching for the veil.

The young man tossed it at Morgan and sank back to the floor, facing away from him. Morgan quickly pulled it across his mouth, letting it cover his lips, and latched it around his head. It made him feel normal, but it was silly. The veil shouldn't have mattered.

"I'm Finley. You can call me Fin if you want—

everyone does," the young man said, staring at the Divine heraldry hung on the wall. It matched the one on the chair; twin chrysanthemums done in blackwork with a golden sun behind them. "Divine Morgan, right?" He glanced over his shoulder, a small tilt to his lips like a shy smile. "It's always nice to know your mouth is as normal as mine."

Morgan eyed him. "I have sharp teeth. That's not as normal as yours." Fin chuckled, shrugging, and Morgan drew his knees closer. A glimmer of color caught his eye and he looked; some of the baubles he'd hung up were smashed on the floor.

Somehow, it hurt. Even if he didn't remember who'd given him the glass orbs. Fin followed his gaze and his face fell. He went over to the nearest pile of shards and attempted to pick them up.

"I'm so sorry," he said quietly. "I'll—uh—I'll—"

"It's fine." Morgan tightened his arms around his knees and averted his gaze. "What were you doing on the roof?"

Fin swallowed, leaving the glass where it was, and scrubbed his hands on his trousers. He took another moment, like he was searching for the words, and faced Morgan properly. "I was looking for your room, actually. Just didn't mean to fall through the roof."

Morgan's heart skipped and forced himself to

ignored the first part of the sentence—no one was ever looking for him. "H-How did you get to the roof?" he asked. Instead of looking right at Fin, he focused on his veil; something felt wrong. It was crooked. With an inaudible sigh, he reached back for the clasp to fix it.

"I climbed," Fin said, sounding taken aback. "Guess I missed your window. Sorry." He smiled apologetically and hesitated before continuing. "You don't have to wear the veil if you don't want to. I didn't mean to make you uncomfortable and throw it at you." Morgan ceased fidgeting with the clasp. "I won't tell anyone."

It *was* silly. Fin had already seen Morgan without it and hadn't burst into flames.

"You know," Fin continued, "at school, we were taught the Lord of Night would smite anyone who looked upon his Divine with familiarity." He drummed his fingers on his knees and then grinned, like a thought struck him at once. "It must not be true. Nothing's punished me yet."

Morgan snorted back a chuckle and dropped the veil in his lap. It still felt weird, somehow bare to the world—even if the world was a single person—but it was freeing. The small smile made his lips sting and he gently ran his tongue across the bitemark he must have left. Blood. Alarmed, he ran the back of his hand across his mouth; it came away red. There were even splotches of blood on the veil.

Frustration etched into his thoughts, blooming a headache behind his eyes. "Why are you here?" Morgan asked, praying the question took attention away from him trying to rub out the blood.

"I wanted to talk to you," Fin said, drumming his fingers along his knees again. "I tried to go through the clergy, but they told me to get lost. Never liked me much anyway." He cleared his throat, like he was brushing the fact away. "My dad called and told me about you being in Rosenburg for a sending or... a couple sendings, I guess. I figured I'd be able to catch you before you got into solitude, but they kinda shoved you in here pretty quick."

Morgan stopped trying to rub the blood out—he was just making it worse—and narrowed his eyes. "You still haven't said *why* you're here."

"Sorry. I'm nervous. This sounds so silly in my head." Fin sighed, a great heave from his chest like he tried to breathe out his nerves. "My grandmother died."

Flickers of memory reacted to how sad he sounded. Like they wanted to soothe his worries away. They were from earlier in the week, before Morgan had left for Rosenburg, leaving them fuzzy and soft around the edges now. An old woman smiling at herself in the mirror. Her silver hair braided across her head, prim and proper. Then she was smiling at a young man in the kitchen—her grandson. Familial love washed over Morgan and his heart ached.

"Yes," Morgan said, letting the memories fade. Fin watched him, hopeful. "I remember her. Beatrice Thorne, right?" Fin nodded. "I've already sent her."

"I know," Fin whispered, cutting his gaze away. "I just... I wanted to know if she wanted to tell me something before she passed. It felt like she wanted to, but she could barely speak in the end and-and I just wanted to see if I was right."

He'd said it all incredibly fast, words smashed together like he wanted to speed past his vulnerability. His voice grew quieter by the end, a soft whisper like he might have been wrong. Morgan didn't blame him. He turned to his desk, where his mess still lay, ignored. Her scroll was nestled in the shelves beside the other ones he hadn't proffered to the clergy yet.

Morgan stood and on his way over to the desk, retrieved the scalpel and shoved it into his pocket. He was all too aware of the way Fin watched him, curious and like he wanted to say something, but Morgan was glad he never did.

The scroll whispered to Morgan; it knew he wanted to check on it. The memories embedded in the ink and the soft touch of the primordial hymn pulled him closer until he gently unfurled it. Fin came up beside him and leaned in to read.

Morgan tried not to be distracted, but it was painfully hard with Fin so close to him. He was taller than Morgan thought—Morgan barely reached past his shoulders—and smelled faintly of oranges and pines.

No. He had to concentrate. Morgan forced his eyes to the scroll.

The details he'd written were sparse. Beatrice hadn't left behind many of her memories. Her soul had been like water, never settling like she was the waves of the ocean, until Morgan hummed with her. Then her soul had calmed and nestled into his hands, soft and warm. Like a hug.

Fin was trying to read over his shoulder, mouthing syllables, but Morgan shook his head. "This version is written in a dialect only for clergy," Morgan said.

"Oh."

"And not very helpful." Morgan rolled it up and reaffixed the red thread. He slid it back to its home and studied Fin a moment longer before continuing. "Did you want me to check her again? Has she been buried?"

"Not yet," Fin said. "It's mourning week still." He

tilted his head toward Morgan. "The clergy said they don't allow for second checks."

"I never said I didn't," Morgan said. "I'm still new at this. I could have missed it."

Even though he'd just admitted a grievous fault, Fin's eyes lit up. Morgan's heart skipped, his face flushing. The smile was warm, eager, and incredibly infectious. For some reason, Morgan remembered tracing it softly with his fingers.

"You'd really do that?" Fin said.

Morgan nodded, shaking the image of Fin's lips from his mind and faced the desk. "I have four more days of solitude." He turned and watched the door. Still no voices and the cord remained intact. Fin followed his gaze, lifting his eyebrows. "If no one heard you fall in, they won't know I'm gone."

Fin smiled even wider. "I can get you down and back before they even realize it."

An adventure. Morgan's pulse buzzed just thinking about it. He'd leave the priory as Morgan, not as the Divine. He found a soft smile stretching across his lips.

"Yes... but—" He slid his hands underneath his hair and Fin looked at it. The snow-white strands indicative of the Divine. "What about this? Someone's going to notice."

Fin was already stripping off his jacket before

Morgan finished and threw it over him. Honestly, given how quickly he had it off, he might have been more excited for the escape than Morgan. The hood covered the hair just fine and Fin helped Morgan pull it on. Though oversized, it was soft, warm, and smelled like spices. He stopped himself from breathing it in too deeply—he wanted to be normal—and Fin readjusted the hood, tucking Morgan's hair gently behind his ears.

The touch made Morgan impossibly warm and Fin quickly retracted his hands, like even he realized what he was doing was too intimate. Morgan finished hiding his hair on his own as Fin headed back to the window.

"W-Wait. I can't climb," Morgan said with sudden realization. He paused pulling on the boots he'd grabbed from his wardrobe. "I'm sorry."

"I can!" Fin snickered as Morgan gave him a look—of course *he* could climb. "Bet I can climb down with you hanging off my back. You're not heavy."

Morgan's heart skipped. Maybe he was afraid of heights. Yes. That must have been it. No other reason for his heart to suddenly do the flutter it had been doing since Fin emerged from the mess. He stared at the door, straining his ears. No one was coming to investigate. He surely would have heard them by now. Small miracles.

And it dawned on him: he really *could* escape.

Morgan shared a warm smile with Fin. "Let's go."

It didn't take long to get situated against Fin's back. Without his jacket, Morgan saw how lean Fin's arms and back were beneath his tank top and quite honestly, it was a little distracting. Morgan did his best to ignore it to keep from embarrassing himself to death, and wrapped his arms around Fin's neck while Fin helped him get his legs across his torso to make sure he didn't fall.

Fin threw one leg out the window and Morgan caught sight of his blanket underneath all the debris on his bed. Panic jolted through him. "Wait!" he squeaked and Fin paused. "Wait. Let me down."

Fin settled back inside the room, eyebrows drawn together in confusion, and Morgan scrambled off his back—nearly falling if not for Fin catching him at the last minute. He hurried over to the bed and pulled his blanket free.

"This is silly," Morgan said, cheeks warm as he folded it. "Can I take this? I can't bear leaving it here. It's actually mine."

"Of course." Fin helped Morgan search the room for a bag to put it in. They found one in the wooden chest at the end of the bed, underneath Morgan's old clothes, and he slipped the blanket safely inside.

"Thank you," Morgan whispered and they situated themselves to leave again.

Fin expertly swung them out of the window, Morgan hanging on for dear life, and Morgan only opened his eyes once Fin began descending.

There were grooves in the spire wall, perfectly spaced apart for climbing, and Morgan now under-stood how Fin had accidentally gone to the roof. The grooves continued all the way up, like someone had used them once upon a time to sit up there. Morgan traced a groove with his finger as they passed. Little glimmers of memory were imbedded within each one. Maybe another Divine had escaped the same way during their days of solitude. Or perhaps more than that. Night after night, escaping to be them-selves and not the Divine. Morgan wished he'd looked before now; then again, he wasn't sure if he would have been brave enough to climb on his own, especially since he hardly had the same deftness Fin had as he descended.

They reached the bottom before long, neither making an attempt to fill the silence with noise. Morgan was glad; it let him concentrate on how sure Fin was and how exact he was with climbing instead of how high they were. Still, Morgan was relieved to feel solid ground beneath his feet. Climbing was not something he wanted to do right away again.

Looking up, seeing how far they'd gone, made his stomach flip.

Fin bent over and picked up an old bike left on the ground, bringing Morgan's attention back to the here and now. The bike was a dusty brown, clearly worn with age, but well-loved. The seat was taped together, the wheels mismatched, but it was a lovely hodgepodge of a bike. Many people in Blackburn rode bikes in lieu of actual vehicles because the streets were packed so tightly together. Bikes just made sense.

"I can ride us both down." Fin patted the rear bike rack. "Just sit here and hold onto me."

Morgan had never ridden a bike before, but it wasn't too awkward as he adjusted himself on the back. At least, until holding onto Fin's waist crossed his mind. For some reason, it made Morgan's entire body warm. Even warmer when Fin tired of waiting and pulled Morgan's arms around his waist.

"There. Just like that," Fin said, giving them a gentle pat.

There was no more time to feel embarrassed when Fin took off. His legs powered the pedals faster than Morgan thought he'd go at first and Morgan squeezed his arms tighter, pressing himself flush against Fin's back as he shut his eyes. The path back to the main road was bumpy, little ditches here and there that Fin dodged with ease. Once they were on the road though, it smoothed and Morgan risked opening his eyes.

The priory sped away from them, disappearing behind the throng of trees and past the twists and turns of the road. It was steep, once a road the devout traversed on their pilgrimages from priory to priory, but it had since been paved for cabs and the like to help the devout make the route much easier if they even bothered. As it was, Fin didn't even have to pedal once they got going.

The wind whipped through them and Morgan struggled to keep the hood over his hair. He didn't mind; it felt like he was alive. He relaxed against Fin's back, releasing a soft sigh, and let himself smile as the summer air whistled through him.

IV.

GRANDMOTHER

The ride from the priory was more exhilarating than any cab ride had ever been and Morgan couldn't stop smiling. Trees flew by, a blur of soft greens and yellows, and then so did Blackburn as they whizzed into town. Few places were open this late, not like Rosenburg. The streets there had been teeming with life underneath the evening sun while Blackburn was sleepy in comparison. What remained opened were the few shops along the main thoroughfare and a late afternoon farmer's market in the center of town.

Fin sped by the dwindling crowds all the same, not even glancing at anyone who might have called his name. Morgan still ducked his head when they neared others, clutching the hood tighter over his head, but who in their right mind would steal the Divine from the priory? No one would believe such a thing possible even if they *had* caught the glimmer of white hair underneath Morgan's hood.

The roads leading away from the main thoroughfare were like veins in the body; small and winding, they spread between the houses and establishments throughout Blackburn. The road Fin chose brought them past a library proudly proclaiming itself as old as the priory, a school closed for the evening, and a myriad of little businesses before they came to the swathes of houses on the outer reaches of Blackburn.

The houses were all different shapes and sizes, some new, some old, and most of them completely lived in for generations. The older ones had modernization tacked on as an afterthought, many times as a mess of wires connected from the house to the poles on the street. Most even had carports awkwardly jutting off the side to cover vehicles the residents managed to squeeze down the streets. The houses were a mishmash of every single era of modernization as Blackburn raced to keep up. A constant cycle of rebirth of its own.

Fin took them past the newer homes, past some of the not as old ones, and kept pedaling. Part of Morgan wanted to ask exactly *where* Fin's grandmother's house was, but he feared it would ruin the sense of adventure.

They slowed when they passed through a small thicket of trees growing close to the road. Beyond it was almost idyllic; the evening sun shone on grass overgrown with wildflowers, the houses were spaced farther apart than those before with lush wildflower gardens between them, and all Morgan wanted to do was lay down in the flowers and breathe them in.

There was one house at the end of the lane, far enough apart from the others to be a little more private. Pine trees nestled around it protectively, casting soft shadows across the yard. The exterior was well-kept with rust red bricks paired with dark green wooden accents around the windows. The enclosed wooden porch had a rocking chair inside facing outward and potted plants along the exterior of late summer blossoms and early autumn ones beginning to bud. The door was a dark green like the accents with a vibrant wreath of flowers resting above the door knocker. Beside the door was a large window with sheer curtains beyond the glass. Against the side of the house was a rickety carport with a small vehicle safely underneath.

"My grandma's lived here ever since she got married," Fin said, a little breathless, and his voice broke the timeless silence. "Always said she never wanted to live anywhere else."

"I see that," Morgan said. The house had trickles of her memories all over it, blossoming a distinct emotion not his own in the back of his mind. Something like pride. The house had been built just for her and her husband as a wedding gift from her father. Even all these years later, it stood the test of time and weathered whatever life had thrown at it.

They took the bike into the porch and left it beside the rocking chair. The one Fin's grandmother must have sat in countless times. Morgan felt her all over it. The way she'd watch Fin play outside when he was little. How she watched the morning there with a cup of tea resting on her knee. Even reading as the sun went down before she had to call Fin inside.

Morgan shook the memories from his head and stood beside Fin. He hadn't reached to open the door yet, so they lingered. A little longer than Morgan thought they would have, but then Fin released a long sigh and let them in.

The door opened to the scent of funeral herbs, what the clergy used to preserve the body for the week of mourning. The woody scent of myrrh mixed with cassia that Morgan had become accustomed to. Shortly after death, the body was cleaned, dressed with herbs to preserve the body, and clothed in something the deceased would have loved to wear. Bodies were given a wicker coffin and then sent home to begin the week of mourning. As such, most viewings took place in the home, specifically the foyer. At least, that was the case in Blackburn. Morgan had heard Rosenburg had dedicated buildings for viewings now because houses were being built too small to accommodate them.

The foyer had been cleaned out of its usual coats and shoes. Chrysanthemums replaced them instead, each one carefully tacked to the hooks to the point of overflowing. Their hues were gold, red, and white to match the colors on the Divine's ceremonial robes. Petals had already fallen to the floor, coating the walkway in colors, and it was customary to leave them where they fell because it symbolized the dead returning one last time to visit.

Personal photos had been carefully taped to the wall between the chrysanthemum bundles. Of friends and family, many with Fin's grandmother in the center. Morgan gazed at each one, piecing together the woman he'd seen glimpses of within her own memories. Though there were many without, there were just as many with Fin brightly smiling beside her. He'd started small, all baby fat making his cheeks round, and then he grew up, ending up at least a head taller than her, but he kept the same smile on his lips. In one of the photos near the end of her life, he had an arm wrapped happily around her as she leaned into him with a bright, proud smile upon her lips.

Fin stood beside the coffin at the back of the foyer already; he hadn't lingered like Morgan had. The coffin had been set horizontally against the small shrine everyone had in their homes of the Lord and Lady. Typically, the shrine was a small alcove with a simple pictograph of the gods within where people would light candles during equinoxes and solstices to provide light for the gods in case they visited. Right now, it was covered because of the coffin.

"Tomorrow," Fin broke the silence and crossed his arms tightly. "T-Tomorrow is her actual burial." He wiped his cheeks and leaned against the wall beside him. "I'm glad you said yes."

So was Morgan. Before he'd departed for Rosenburg, he'd noticed a flurry of activity in the priory, one befitting the prep of a burial and thought nothing of it. The cemetery was close to the priory, a green glade around a flowering tree, signifying the dead's eventual rebirth. Morgan had loved sitting out there on slow days until the Head Prior grew worried his immaculate presence would deter loved ones from visiting.

Morgan forced himself to focus and peered into the wicker coffin to really look at Beatrice. A flower crown caught his attention first; it was made of red and gold chrysanthemums and pinned to the silver braid drawn across her head. Her face was still, the small smile on her lips coated in red lipstick. Someone had even given her cheeks color, something subtle so she wasn't so pale. This almost felt fake. She wasn't smiling before.

He kept the thought to himself.

Instead of the linen hospital gown she'd been in when Morgan saw her in the priory sending room, she now wore a beautiful ruby red dress with white lace decorating the neckline. Beatrice's favorite. Someone had drawn a pale violet blanket across her from the waist down, like she would have been cold otherwise, and it was embroidered with flowers. Her hands sat upon the edge of the blanket, clasped together, and her gold wedding ring was in full view.

She was still. Silent. Not at all alive like in her memories. Not the vibrant woman she'd been. It wasn't a shock to Morgan—this was how she was in the sending room, after all—but for some reason, he'd expected her to be exactly the same as in her memories. Her complete stillness and silence left Morgan unsettled. Like it was the first time he'd seen a dead body—but it wasn't.

He shouldn't have been unsettled at all. The morgue in Rosenburg was unsettling. It was silent in a way here wasn't, traumatized with death. Here, it was something soft and inviting. Personal and close. Peaceful, like death should have been. Maybe it was because he'd left his robe and veil at the priory. Staring at the dead, leaving himself open and uncovered, just felt wrong.

He watched Beatrice, willing himself to calm down and remember the one simple truth he knew: Divines weren't holy because of the robe and veil. They were holy because they were touched by the Lord of Night. The affirmation calmed Morgan's heart and he shoved his doubts somewhere far away where it was a whisper so he could focus.

It helped Fin had stayed quiet. The slow, rhythmic melody of his breathing helped Morgan settle even more. It mixed with the soft song slowly rising up from Beatrice.

Breathing in deep, Morgan got to work. He left his bag with Fin and reached into the coffin. He pressed his fingers against the middle of her chest, where her heart had been. There was a tingle against his skin, and he followed it to her neck, where her pulse would have been. A shimmer passed over his fingers and he blinked. Something *was* there.

And he'd missed it at the priory.

She'd been hesitant to leave her body even then and by the time the entire process was over, Morgan had been exhausted. He hadn't thought he *could* leave something behind. It was so subtle too, Morgan wondered if it had simply bloomed inside her because she was home. A piece of her was in everything around them, after all, and now that her body was empty with the smallest bit of her soul left, those pieces returned to settle within her once more.

He leaned in farther, reaching for the hymn souls always sang, and pressed his lips to her cold cheek. The effect was immediate. Grainy and soft memories overcame his, barely whole. A child smiled up at her, gap toothed, and held tight to her hand. Next, she was teaching the child to cook. He'd needed a footstool to reach the stove. Then she sat at his bedside, weaving a story of queens, kings, and knights. The child watched her with wonder sparkling in his eyes, a plush rabbit tight in his arms.

Each soft memory was tinged with sadness and whispered feelings through Morgan's entire being. She'd never felt it was her place to raise Fin, but his father was too busy and the boy had been a handful without his mother. But she'd done her best by him and would do it all over again if she had the choice. The memories shifted and more and more, as Morgan watched Fin grow up and Beatrice grow old, the sadness replaced itself with pride.

The last memory attached to the house was a quiet moment between Beatrice and Fin over tea. A conversation unsaid. And then she looked right at Morgan. It made his heart jolt, but she only smiled as soft words whispered a melody from her lips.

"Thank you," Beatrice said, washing warmth throughout Morgan's entire being. It suddenly felt like she stood beside him. "I know he's been fretting, but tell him I am proud of him and I'll always be proud, no matter what he's done. He deserves to know before I enter the arms of the Lord of Night."

Hands touched Beatrice's over Morgan's. He hadn't even realized he'd covered them until then and he flinched, opening his eyes. The Lord of Night stared at him, warm hands clasped atop Morgan's. It was a glimpse, the Lord's snow-white hair cascading over his shoulders, his eyes as black as the night sky, and Morgan jerked backwards. The Lord disappeared, taking the warmth of his hands with his image. Morgan would have fallen outright, trying to drag himself back to reality, if Fin hadn't swung a strong arm across his back to catch him.

Memories folded in on themselves, sliding free, and Fin's form shuddered beside him. A child in one blink, then the young man he was now. He oscillated between reality and memory and Morgan forced his mind to settle on reality, even as everything grew fuzzy and out of reach.

"What?" Fin asked, his voice grounding Morgan.

The foyer stopped spinning so swiftly, Morgan feared falling, but Fin remained constant. A steady pillar holding him up. Warm.

"Nothing," Morgan said, pushing the word out through a lump in his throat. He shook the glimpse of the Lord of Night free from his thoughts and breathed in deep. The Lord must have sensed Morgan's poor job at sending Beatrice's soul and came to check in. Close enough to the equinox, so it was possible. That was all. Nothing more. Morgan didn't even have to ingest the soul this time. It was a blessing.

"She—she—" Morgan squeezed his eyes shut, swallowing. His body was finally revolting from the complete lack of food. Lack of sleep. He was getting so dizzy just standing there. "She said she was proud of you." Morgan forced the words front and center in his thoughts. He didn't want to forget them. Not yet. "And she always will be. No matter what you've done."

Fin's face softened as he watched Morgan.

"She thought you deserved to know," Morgan continued, grasping at the words as they continued to fade into the haze of memory. That was it. He righted himself and tried to breathe evenly. "I'm sorry." He wrapped his arms around himself. "I should have seen this."

Fin still smiled softly at him. "It's all right. I bet they rushed you. Everything's always strict and by the book there, no accounting for any diversion souls might take."

Maybe they *had* rushed him. Or maybe the memories simply waited for the body to return home before making themselves known. He'd never know.

The room shimmered and Morgan squeezed his eyes shut. His memories blurred over. All he could think of were her words, her memories, and bit by bit, he saw himself in her place. It was too much. He wasn't himself. He was losing himself each damn time. All he could think was how she loved her house, loved her grandson, loved her life. How she sat in the morning sun, drinking her tea and watching the world roll by. How *he* used to paint in his younger years.

It wasn't him. No. He'd never painted. He'd never picked up a brush, but it felt like he had. He knew the strokes. He knew how to mix all the colors he'd ever used. But it was all Beatrice. Her memories were too stark and intimate. He needed himself back.

My name is Morgan, he told himself, stressing the

syllables in his head. *My mother's name is... Cynthia. My father's name is Charles.* No. That wasn't right. Morgan tried harder to remember. *Joseph.* No. No. It wasn't even that. He squeezed his eyes tighter, holding his head. No. The name was gone. So far gone, he'd simply assigned his father a new name. No face surfaced. No comforting smile to assuage him out of his breakdown. It was gone. Completely gone and he'd let it go.

"Hey." Fin's hand warmed his shoulder so suddenly and real, Morgan flinched away, clattering against the wall.

Reality returned in a rush, making his empty stomach churn. Fin remained the same as ever, but there was a flicker of flame behind him. No. Not real. It wasn't there. It was never there.

"Are you okay?" Fin asked.

"No," Morgan whispered before he could lie—pretend—believe his own lie. Tears spilled out of his eyes so suddenly, he couldn't stop them. "Nothing's okay," he strained. The tears dripped down to his chin. "I am not me anymore. All I am is this *thing* to pull memories from the dead. I can't—I can't do this anymore." He closed his eyes, whispering a plea as fire coated him. It snaked through the foyer despite the plea, turning the petals into floating embers, and bit by bit, the wicker coffin went aflame.

"No one cares. I'm *just* the Divine," Morgan cried. "I can't even remember my parents' faces. Barely even their names." Morgan looked at his hands. They were pale, foreign, and his vision blurred with more tears. "I barely even remember myself and no one cares."

Suddenly realizing it was still there, Morgan shot his hand into his pocket and pulled the scalpel free. An escape, another variety, and he quickly ended those thoughts by handing it to Fin. He'd already seen it. He'd probably already guessed why Morgan had it at all, even if he'd never verbally admit it. Just to save Morgan from having to confess it aloud.

"I'm sorry," Morgan whispered and scrubbed his cheeks. "I didn't..." He breathed out, trying to piece broken words together. "I didn't mean to tell you all that. Your grandmother deserved the job done right. She was a good person." He stared up at the ceiling; anything but to look at Fin. "I shouldn't have said anything."

"Why not?" Fin asked. "It's what you're feeling." His voice was soft, almost a murmur. Like a voice he'd heard before. Early in the morning before anyone should have been in his room. He remembered so faintly how he'd leaned into the voice as it soothed any lingering nightmare away.

Morgan refused to lean closer this time; he

didn't know Fin. That was someone else's memory. The voice was not and never was Fin. "You're entitled to be yourself," Fin continued in the same voice. "All the messy feelings included."

"No." Morgan shook his head. "It's made this harder. What if something I feel ends up in their memories? Their soul? What if I misremember something?" More tears threatened to fall and he blinked them back. Fin didn't answer. Morgan was right. He wasn't *really* Divine; just a poor imitation that never should have been. He exhaled deeply. "I shouldn't even *be* here."

He screwed everything up. What if those hadn't actually been her words? What if Morgan had made them up because he wanted them to mean something to Fin? He'd never know. His heart hammered against his chest, winding up in panic, and he could barely stay still as his entire body trembled.

"You don't want to be *there*," Fin said and Morgan only peered at him when something clattered across the floor. Fin had tossed the scalpel into the kitchen; Morgan couldn't see where it had gone. Out of sight; out of mind. "Don't sell your feelings short." Fin refused to break eye contact. "You were happy on the way down. Have you ever smiled as Divine?"

The question was so familiar, it struck Morgan like an arrow to his chest. He stared at Fin, his eyes wide, trying to piece together some memory sunk so far below all the others. Someone had asked him the very same, but his memories wouldn't give up who.

"I can take you back," he said quietly. "Now—if you want. I appreciate you coming out here like this." He drew closer, only stopping when Morgan tensed. "Do you want to go back?"

Morgan leaned against the wall again, something to prop him up when his legs wanted so badly to fold underneath him. "I don't know," he whispered.

Going back meant facing the Head Prior and lying about the ceiling once someone actually noticed. Meant facing the memories of fire just waiting to overcome him because of the scroll with no name. It meant going back to everything undoing him.

Fin watched him, like staring would produce some other answer, but Morgan let his indecision hang in the air between them. It was all he had.

"How about this?" Fin's voice bridged them back together, light and soft. "Let me cook you something nice for dinner as thanks." He was smiling again when Morgan lifted his gaze. "I can run by the market, pick up something good. And we can sit together. Be friends." He paused, like he wanted to say something else too, but changed his mind mid-breath. "And we can keep my grandma company a little while longer."

A home-cooked meal. It warmed something cold and distant in Morgan's chest. His lips twitched into a fleeting smile. "I'd like that."

His weak reply was all the confirmation Fin needed; he shuffled Morgan up through the kitchen threshold, taking him away from Beatrice, and settled Morgan's bag on the table. He promised to be back soon and was out the door, pedaling away, before Morgan had a chance to suggest he could go with.

Instead, he sat alone at the table in a kitchen he'd never known, but somehow knew exactly where everything was.

V.
WREATHED IN THE PINES

It wasn't long before all earlier doubt and panic ebbed back, stealing away the soft acceptance the kitchen had been steeped in.

Morgan shouldn't have said yes. He was intruding. Maybe he could walk back to the priory on his own. Surely, they'd noticed he was gone by now and would meet him halfway back, but the more Morgan listened to the silence around him, the more he wasn't so sure. The priory had a siren they played for dangerous weather and the like and if they'd found him missing, surely, they'd use it to alert the citizens of Blackburn *something* was wrong.

But it never came. Crickets sung in the blooming twilight and the wind brushed past the pine trees, blowing a faraway wind chime.

Still, something deep down told him he shouldn't have been in someone's house by himself.

"And why not?"

Morgan jolted. The kitchen had grown fuzzy with a golden shroud cast over everything in the evening haze. He blinked. A woman sat across from him, wearing Beatrice's vibrant dress, but was decades younger. Thick brown hair just like Fin's. Sun-soaked skin from days spent in her garden painting away. Beatrice in the prime of her life.

No. This wasn't real. She wasn't there.

"You've been invited," Beatrice said, her tone the same as he'd heard in her memories. The soft lilt of her voice made him warm inside. "Stay a while. Nothing will harm you here."

He was delusional. His mind had finally broken and gave up trying to piece together who he was, instead smashing him together with what remained of Beatrice. Except he couldn't deny how comfortable her invitation made him. His heart calmed considerably and his thoughts slowed. Beatrice moved from her seat, a shimmer left in her wake, and she fussed about the kitchen. Like an impression of herself lasting throughout time itself.

The kitchen was small. Old appliances, cupboards worn with time, but somehow just right in a house steeped in some distant memory. The dining table had a lace tablecloth spread across it and in the center lay a funeral bouquet, its flowers abloom as a sea of reds and golds.

A tea cup placed itself in front of him, set down by a ghostly hand.

Warm with the fragrance of orange blossom, the tea sent a tingle throughout his body as he sipped it. Had he made it, or had Fin left it for him and he didn't register it until now? His head throbbed and as he tried to piece together something that made sense, the same hand gently led him out of the kitchen and into the living room.

A large bay window sat at one end, overlooking the yard behind the house, and let in the soft evening light. It shone over the couch set against the staircase on one side, a knitted blanket spread across its back, and the couch faced the fireplace across from it. Two arm chairs flanked the couch and a coffee table sat in the center of it all. Stuffed in one corner was a small entertainment stand with an old television sitting on top with its steel antennas reaching up toward the ceiling while in the other corner was a bookcase filled to the brim with all sorts of differently shaped books.

What drew Morgan's gaze last and held it the longest was the painting above the fireplace. The Lady of Dawn had been lovingly depicted, her honey brown hair drawn in a braid crowning her head, and she was wreathed in sunflowers. It was such a serene, intimate portrait. And he felt his hands paint it. No. Not his. Beatrice's. She'd loved all the old pictographs around the priory and wanted to make one herself.

The priory never accepted it, even when she'd offered, because the Lady of Dawn was above all. Not something that amounted to a personal piece. Beatrice hadn't minded; the painting had made its home above the fireplace instead and welcomed all who sat inside the living room. Like Morgan.

The same hands which painted such an intimate portrait led him to the couch. They tucked him underneath the blanket and a kiss was gently placed on his head. She whispered a song, one so ingrained in Morgan's mind, he hummed back until it was only his voice in the silence. The vibration from his throat reminded him he was real. Himself still.

The door opened, the sound distant, and stole the shroud over the room. Morgan had hardly sat himself up before Fin came through the kitchen doorway, panicked. He exhaled once he noticed Morgan in the dim light and smiled again.

"You tired?" he asked, returning to flick on the light in the kitchen.

"I always am after a sending," Morgan said,

resting his eyes. "I'll get up."

"Nah, stay there!" Fin called out. "I'll let you know when I'm done. Vegetables all right with you? I got a good assortment cheap."

"I like vegetables," Morgan whispered, forcing his eyes back open. He didn't want to fall asleep just yet and busied himself by watching Fin's shadow as he moved about.

"Want to watch TV?" Fin asked.

Morgan glanced at the television in the corner. The priory had one in the room clergypersons typically congregated in when they weren't needed, but he'd never used it himself. "It's fine. I wouldn't know what to watch."

"Also got a radio somewhere in there."

Up on the top of the bookshelf, but Morgan shook his head. "I'm fine," he repeated.

Only when Fin began humming as he cooked did Morgan realize perhaps Fin liked noise in the background while he worked. Too late now, Morgan supposed. The melody coming from Fin was something a little broken and meandering, but soft enough that Morgan honestly expected to be lulled back to sleep, especially as it paired itself with the ambient noises of cooking and the soft sounds from outside. As he felt himself begin to drift off, Fin spoke, breaking the spell.

"How old are you, anyway?"

Morgan blinked, glancing toward the kitchen. "Seventeen. I was born around the Hibernal Solstice."

"Ah. Handy way to remember. Do they celebrate your birthday up there?"

Morgan shrugged, settling his head back into the couch cushion. "I received a small cake last year. They don't usually make sweets, so it was actually rather kind of them."

It had been a yellow cake with fluffy white frosting all over it. Someone had placed strawberries along the top, each one cut into the shape of hearts. No one admitted to making it and it had shown up on his desk while he was out of his room. Morgan doubted even the Head Prior had known about it. He'd savored each bite, hardly wanting to finish it because then it meant it'd be gone.

"Think I can make you a cake this year? Bet I could climb with a cake."

Morgan couldn't hide his smile imagining it and was glad Fin couldn't see it. If he'd still be around then, if he'd still know Fin then, he wanted so badly to say yes. But he didn't want to get his hopes up. He stayed quiet instead.

Another stretch of silence eased between them until Fin asked, "What's your favorite color?"

Morgan snorted and glared at Fin from the

couch, only to turn away, flushing, once Fin peeked inside with a grin. "I don't—"

"I know. Memory and all that." Fin returned to the stove. Something was sizzling in the pan. A sharp flavor with a medley of vegetables. "I think talking would help. If you had to choose a color right now, what would you pick?"

Morgan settled back against the couch in thought. He gently touched the cord still around his waist. He'd always liked how vibrant it was. "Red."

"Hey—me too!"

Fin didn't ask anything else and just as Morgan went to ask one of his own, Fin came in with two bowls in hand. He set them on the coffee table with a flourish, and Morgan couldn't help the soft chuckle escaping his throat, especially when Fin winked at him. After flipping on a lamp, illuminating the warm hues in the living room, Fin retreated again into the kitchen, going back for drinks. Morgan's stomach growled as he breathed in the aroma and pushed himself up to sit properly on the couch.

Simmered vegetables stewed in something Morgan couldn't guess, but it reminded him of ginger, with bites of cooked chicken sprinkled throughout, and it was all heaped on a large bowl of brown rice.

Fin returned with their drinks and sat beside

Morgan as he set them down. There was enough space between them, like it was intentional, and Morgan tried not dwelling on it, instead looking into the cups. It was some kind of fruit juice, sweet to the taste. Morgan took a tentative bite from his bowl and could barely help himself as he shoveled more in. It was amazing.

"Did you have any friends at the priory?" Fin asked.

Morgan wasn't as defensive with food in his stomach; he chewed on a mouthful and gave the question some real thought. A young woman came to mind. He couldn't remember her name—it was long gone by now—but he remembered details vividly among the other memories vying for his attention. She had thick black curls framing her face, skin a russet brown with freckles like Fin's, and had always worn thick, black framed glasses.

"Sort of," Morgan said, pushing around his rice. "Divines have attendants—basically partners for travel and someone to do all the boring priory stuff with—and they always try to pair Divines with attendants close in age, for comradery I guess." He shrugged. "They have trouble finding attendants for me since I'm so young. They've given up trying. Usually when I need one, a regular clergyperson volunteers, but it's not the same."

Fin nodded, mouth full of food, and waved at him to continue.

"I don't remember her very well," Morgan admitted. "It was maybe two years ago? She loved telling me stories as she helped me around the priory. Eventually, she was giving me books she smuggled inside." He chuckled at the memory of her pulling a thick tome from underneath her clergy robes so he could read it. "Sometimes I wondered if she took them from the library—so many had Blackburn and an address stamped inside. I learned so much from them and she was happy to talk to me about the plots and nuances." He trailed off slowly, his heart aching.

Fin swallowed his food, a distant look in his eyes. "I take it the prior wasn't happy when he learned that," he whispered. "Ideas are dangerous for a young Divine."

Morgan nodded. "She left. They told me she'd decided clergy life wasn't for her. I was hurt at the time, but as the months went by, I think I realized it wasn't her choice." He sighed. "I took the books and buried them in the priory garden. I'd memorized them and I didn't want to get in trouble. I left a note hidden in the wardrobe for any Divine after me, though, just in case they needed the escape too."

In truth, he couldn't bear to look at the books

after she'd left. A painful reminder he wasn't allowed to actually have friends. He was the Divine. Untouchable. Above everything else.

They stayed quiet for a time before Fin spoke again. He'd finished his bowl, every last grain of rice, and set it on the coffee table.

"Your lip okay?" he asked.

Morgan ran his tongue across it. Still stung, but the bleeding had ceased a while ago. "It's fine."

Fin leaned back, eyes on Morgan's lips and Morgan grew warm. He shoved some more food in his mouth to stop thinking about Fin's lips in return. "How do you deal with those teeth? Do Divines get a crash course or something?"

Morgan laughed, barely having time to swallow his food. "Very carefully." He grinned at Fin, showing off his teeth properly, and Fin snickered.

All at once, Morgan felt as though he'd done the very same before. Sometime, somewhere, he'd shown off his teeth and someone reacted. He wasn't sure *how* they reacted, but it burned something deep in his stomach, making his cheeks grow warmer, and he glanced away. The memory remained stubbornly out of reach and he gave up searching for it. Maybe one day it would be more than a ghost.

"Can I ask you questions now?" Morgan asked.

Fin smirked. "Sure. What'cha got for me?"

"Tell me about yourself," Morgan said. "Were you close to your family?"

Fin made a face and shook his head. "Just my grandma. There's not much to say. Mom didn't actually want kids, but Dad did, so she had one just for him. But she wanted to travel. Couldn't take me, so Dad agreed he'd be fine until she returned." His voice grew quieter with each sentence and Morgan began regretting he'd asked. "Well, she wasn't returning. Dad was stuck with a kid he thought the mom would be around to raise. So, Grandma took me instead and Dad focused on work."

Morgan looked back at his bowl, poking the last few grains of rice with his fork. "Oh."

"He didn't even come down for all this. I had to do all the funeral arrangements," Fin whispered, staring too intently at his bowl. "I was the one ferrying her back and forth from Rosenburg so she could see her doctors. He'd chip in for food and gas, but I don't know." He shrugged and fell back into the couch. "Maybe he couldn't handle the mortality of his own mother and buried himself in work at the morgue. It's what he's good at. Dead are just easier for him to deal with, I guess."

Morgan felt like he should have said something, but all he could think of was apologizing. "I'm sorry," he whispered.

Fin jolted, looking at him suddenly. "No-no, it's all right!" he said quickly. "Lord, I didn't mean to bring the mood down." He nudged Morgan gently. "Don't worry about it. I was here for my grandma, and I think that's what mattered. She did a great job raising me."

"You think so?" Morgan teased.

"Oh, definitely." Fin rolled his eyes and fell back against the couch again. "I always got in trouble when I lived with my dad. Didn't get along with any of the kids in school there and the teachers hated me. Somehow, being out here, I cut it out. People love me here. Besides, it's quiet. Not a lot of opportunity to get into trouble like you can in the city. Still managed it, somehow, but Grandma took it in stride."

"Ah." Morgan slid a glance at him. "So, are you a troublemaker?"

Fin chuckled. "I mean, I did just kidnap the Divine."

Morgan dipped his head to hide his smile. "Is it kidnapping if I came willingly?"

The warm smile on Fin's lips made Morgan's stomach flip and he was glad Fin took it away as he took a drink. "'Sides, I'm energetic. Usually that means getting into trouble. When I graduated, none of the universities in Rosenburg or beyond wanted to deal with me—I'm not smart enough—but I couldn't find an apprenticeship either that wanted to take me. So, I've kinda been stuck here." He rested the glass on his knee. "Last trouble I got into was getting fired from the priory."

Morgan raised his eyebrows. "Really? Why?"

Somehow, the question hurt; Fin winced, but a shrug of his shoulders washed the emotion away. "Just didn't gel with everyone, I guess." He set his glass back on the table. "I've been helping at the library or the school since. If they have stuff to move around, I got the right kind of muscle for the job."

They softly settled into silence and Morgan slowly finished the rest of his bowl. He wasn't sure if he was just biding time until it was completely dark outside, or if he was savoring every last bite because the priory never made anything as delicious. Whichever it was, when he finished, it was dark. The town and priory both would be shuttered until morning. The summer night breeze washed in from the window, cooling everything inside, and Morgan breathed in deep.

"You can stay the night, if you want," Fin said. "I'll ride you back in the morning."

Better than riding in the dark. Morgan nodded and set his bowl beside Fin's.

"You can take my room."

Morgan straightened, his entire body flushing,

and he shook his head. "I couldn't."

Fin was grinning at him, like it was the exact reaction he wanted. "It's comfy, I promise." He stood and gently pulled Morgan up with him. "The couch is not. Believe me. I've crashed on it when I've had friends over. I'd offer my grandma's room... but..."

The reason why floated through them unsaid. She'd died in her room. "Yes," he said, nodding. "That might be unwise."

There was a chance it wouldn't be; Morgan couldn't recall any scripture saying it would be bad for a Divine to rest where someone drew their last breath, but he wasn't in the mood to chance it. He'd had enough of sleepless nights.

Not that he *wanted* to take Fin's room. Before he could reason the couch was just fine, Fin had already led him there. It was across from the staircase off the kitchen. A small space given how tall Fin was, like it had been something entirely different before it became a bedroom.

The bed took the far wall, sitting underneath the window dressed in sheer curtains. It overlooked the pine trees wrapped around the back of the house and the smell of the trees wafted inside freely. Beside the bed was a small desk, much smaller than the one Morgan had in the priory, and atop were opened letters addressed to Fin from someone in Rosenburg.

Beside the pile of letters was what Morgan distantly recalled as a camera. For many sermons, someone from Blackburn would be in the priory taking photos. Most of the time it was a sleeker camera, but sometimes they had one similar to Fin's. It was an off-white in the front and black in the back. There was a single large lens beside a red button and below that was the slot where photos came out of. He'd been fascinated once watching the photographer take pictures, but no one had let him get close to ask how it worked.

He flicked his gaze upward and noticed the photos posted across a corkboard on the wall. Many of them were with friends, with family, and others were of scenic picturesque pastorals all around Blackburn. Each one was taken with care to composition and lighting and Morgan couldn't help but lean in to study them further. He was delighted when he found Fin smiling at him.

"I like photos," Fin said. "Taking them too. I've got my grandma's fancier camera, but I don't have access to a darkroom for processing. This one's an instant camera. Lot faster." He picked up the camera and handed it to Morgan.

As Morgan took it, a shudder worked its way through his fingers. Vestiges of memories came with it, literal snapshots of using it himself once upon a time. Be it as Beatrice, Fin himself, or as someone Morgan didn't know. The memory left as soon as it had sparked. Before he could ask how to use the camera, Fin leaned in beside him and helped lift it so Morgan could see through the viewfinder in the back.

"You aim like this and then press and hold the button," Fin said. "Want me to take your picture?"

"I don't mind," Morgan said, handing it back.

He didn't entirely know how to pose for it as Fin turned the camera on him. Morgan's face bloomed with heat, thinking how silly he must have appeared, and the camera light flashed, sending bright spots across his vision. The photo slid out by the time Morgan could see again and Fin showed him.

Morgan hardly recognized himself still. Yes, there was his white hair. Yes, there was the twinkle of gold in his eyes, even his teeth as his mouth was half-open with a question he hadn't had time to ask. But for some reason, he couldn't say for certain it was him. Like he was still a stranger even to himself.

He must have looked too morose; Fin began fidgeting with the camera, looking like he wanted to ask something, but feared the answer.

"Do you want to be a photographer?" Morgan asked instead, hoping to distract them both.

The fidgeting stopped. "It crossed my mind," Fin

said. "My dad got me in touch with a photographer in the city to show me how to use a darkroom and all that." He resumed fidgeting, not looking at Morgan directly. "I don't think he liked me much; he wouldn't agree to keep teaching me when I finally went back after the priory fired me. Maybe he's too busy. Grandma said I should make a portfolio from what I've done so far—show him I'm serious—but I always get stuck with which photos to put in it. Sometimes, the newspaper here pities me and asks me to take some shots of landscapes and whatnot..."

He was rambling again. Unsure and vulnerable. Morgan wasn't sure what to say and they lapsed into silence until Fin tilted the camera toward him.

"Want to take a picture together?" he asked. "I've got film to spare."

Maybe it would help them both. Morgan nodded, smiling, and couldn't help the butterflies in his stomach when Fin returned it. Fin squeezed in beside him, one arm around his shoulders to keep him still, and perilously held the camera with one hand facing them. Morgan quickly reached up to help steady it, this time remembering to smile, and Fin pressed the button. Morgan was ready for the flash at least, and it didn't take him by surprise. The photo spit out like the first and Morgan took it.

Better. The smile helped, even if it was a little

lopsided and unsure. Morgan couldn't believe he'd forgotten how to smile. He peered at Fin in the photo and his heart thumped. Fin was looking at *him*—not at the camera—with such a soft look on his face. Heat crept up Morgan's cheeks, especially when he realized Fin was looking at the photo with the same expression.

"Hey!" Morgan lifted his eyebrows, trying to act nonplussed. "Why are you looking at me like that?"

Fin blinked and jolted, almost dropping the camera. Morgan covered a laugh as Fin sputtered on a response. "I just... no one usually takes an interest in my photography that much," he said and Morgan wasn't sure if it was the whole truth or not. "You look nice in these. You want to keep them? For when you go back to the priory?"

Thinking of going back gave him a lump in his throat, but he nodded regardless. Even if he scarcely recognized himself, the photos showed him as Morgan, not the Divine. He wanted to keep that.

"All of your pictures are nice." Morgan took the photos from Fin. "Thank you."

The silence was comfortable this time and Morgan took the chance to face the bed. He wasn't getting out of sleeping on it, he figured, with the argument so far gone. Fin had even placed his bag atop it at some point while Morgan had been fascinated with the photos. Morgan reached forward and slid his new memories safely inside the bag.

The bed was soft with a few pillows piled at the headboard and was dressed in a similar blanket to the one resting across Beatrice with the embroidered flowers, except it was red. What drew Morgan's gaze, however, was the stuffed plush rabbit in black overalls nestled against the pillows. The fur was old, clearly loved, and as Morgan reached for it, Fin squeezed past him and snatched it up.

"Ah. Uh." Fin laughed, flustered, and showed it to Morgan. "My mom made me this before she left. He's been with me my whole life."

"He's cute." Morgan gingerly took the rabbit with both hands. He wondered if he'd had something similar once upon a time, but no memories ignited. He held the rabbit closer. "He can sleep here too. Unless—"

"Nope!" Fin said, smiling. "All yours. He's probably tired of me drooling on him." He sucked in a panicked breath as soon as the sentence finished and Morgan raised his eyebrows. "Not that he's been drooled on in a while. He's clean. I swear."

"I suppose I'll have to believe that rambling declaration," Morgan said, chuckling, and avoided Fin's gaze as he grinned at him.

Though Morgan insisted otherwise, Fin also

gave him something old to sleep in. Clothes lost to the flow of time deep in the closet. Just an oversized button-up shirt and shorts, definitely too small for Fin now and hung off Morgan loosely. After showing Morgan where the bathroom was and letting him wash up, Fin bade him goodnight and attempted to close the door behind him as he left the room. Morgan stopped him.

"Leave it open," Morgan said, suddenly embarrassed. Nothing in the dark would get him here, and yet, he didn't want it shut.

"Sure." Fin nodded. At least Morgan didn't have to verbalize why. "I'll leave the light on in the bathroom too. Sleep well, okay? I'll just be out here."

"Good night, Fin," Morgan said.

"Good night, Morgan."

Hearing his name spoken so softly—not Your Holiness or any variation of it—made Morgan's heart flutter. It felt strangely right.

Fin left and Morgan was alone, but it didn't bother him this time. Freedom, in a way. Something so far removed from his priory. He moved his bag to the desk, careful not to disturb the letters or the camera, and pulled his blanket free. He spread it across the top and then crawled underneath it and Fin's blankets. All of it was heavy together and a little warm despite the cool air trickling inside, but he didn't mind. It was a comforting weight, like a hug. He held the rabbit close and breathed in. All he could smell was Fin and it was so calming and familiar, all his worries ceased to exist.

Sleep gently led him under, taking him so deep and through the fires still looming in the fuzzy bits of memories, and he dreamt of nothing at all.

VI.
YEARNINGS OF SUMMER

Morgan roused to sunlight laying over him like a blanket and the murmur of voices floating through the door, piercing through the dregs of sleep. It must have been a busy day at the priory if he could hear the voices up in his room. Someone was coming to wake him any moment now. Maybe he could take that moment to sleep a little longer.

He'd fully intended to, a soft sigh escaping his lips, his eyes falling shut, when he jerked fully awake instead.

This was *not* his room. It smelled nothing like his bed. Far from it. He scrambled upright, heart hammering in his chest, and last evening surged over him in waves. The bike ride down the road—the air whistling past him on his escape—the way

Beatrice had spoken to him—the taste of dinner.

And Fin.

Last night was a whirl, bright, poignant, and something wholly Morgan's in a sea of everything else that distinctly wasn't.

He scrunched up, stuffed rabbit pressed tight against his chest, and listened intently. The voices were quiet, but they argued. None of the words came through clearly, however. All he could tell was one was definitely Fin and the other was someone he hadn't heard before. Morgan frowned. If he'd been caught, then surely the clergy would have already come through the house looking for him. No. It was something else.

Morgan couldn't leave Fin to argue alone; maybe he could help.

Practice walking quietly in the priory came in handy for once; his footsteps were light across the wooden floorboards as he crossed the room and he glanced out the door. No one there and he gently made his way toward the voices in the kitchen.

"Go home, Eryn," Fin said, voice clear over the running of the sink. "I'm completely fine. I promise."

"You practically ran home," the other voice argued, annoyed. "What's going on?"

Morgan crept to the kitchen threshold and peeked inside.

Fin was at the sink with his back to Morgan, washing the dishes they'd used last night. He wore something more formal today; a black collared shirt with a gray vest thrown over top. Morgan even caught the red of a tie around his neck. His trousers matched the shirt and looked stiff, like they weren't worn often, and were paired with black dress shoes. Funeral attire. Always something black with a little red thrown in to symbolize rebirth.

Right. Beatrice's funeral would have been at dawn.

There was a young woman Fin's age near the foyer entrance—she must have been Eryn. She'd puffed up her cheeks, glaring at Fin as if that would make him answer quicker and settled her hands on her hips. She had short red hair in curls crowning her head and like Fin, she wore funeral clothes. A similar collared white shirt with a red ribbon, a black vest trimmed in lace, and a black skirt falling to her knees. Though Fin was tall and lean, she was short and curvy.

She straightened her back, opening her mouth like she'd finally thought of a reply, but suddenly ceased, eyes flicking in Morgan's direction. Morgan had no time to duck back into the living room before their eyes met. She lifted an eyebrow in acknowledgement, gaze darting to his hair and then back to his eyes. Another silent second went by, Fin grumbling at Eryn, and her jaw dropped in recognition.

Fin trailed off, like he noticed the sudden tense air, and turned. His eyes went wide. He jerked between Morgan and Eryn, as though he'd intended to hide Morgan.

"This is my friend!" Fin said. "From Rosenburg. He's staying here for—"

"He's the *Divine*!" Eryn shuffled closer and leaned to one side to look at Morgan unobstructed. "Hi! I'm Eryn!" Her voice was suddenly chipper and she gave him a shy wave.

Morgan waved back. "Um." He swallowed. "P-Please call me Morgan."

She nodded and glared at Fin. "Do you *like* making trouble or something? What made you think this was a good idea?"

Fin had squeezed his eyes shut, pinching the bridge of his nose, and Eryn watched him like she expected an answer. Morgan had no idea what to do; his mind had gone completely blank. The silence grew, turning awkward, and Fin broke it with a long sigh. He undid his tie, set it on the table, and headed for the refrigerator.

"Sit down. Let me cook something while I talk," he said.

His voice was terse, tired, and Morgan wished he hadn't interrupted. He sat as instructed and Eryn followed suit, her gaze never leaving Fin's back. No one spoke as he rummaged through the kitchen to grab the eggs, bread, and some teabags from the pantry. Very soon, the kettle on the stove was filled with water, eggs were sizzling in a pan, and bread was toasting.

When all there was to do was wait, he finally faced them.

"All this week," Fin began haltingly, a soft tremor in his voice, "I thought my grandmother had more to say. It was just a feeling." Eryn's face softened. "Clergy kept saying there were no do-overs on a sending, but I just... I just knew there *had* to be something. So, I asked the Divine himself and he came."

"Oh Fin," Eryn murmured. "Did it help?"

Fin glanced at Morgan briefly, a small smile on his lips. "It did," he whispered before turning his attention back to the food. He turned the eggs over and over, scrambling them in the pan. "I'm taking Morgan back after breakfast. Don't worry; I won't get in trouble again. Clergy won't ever know."

Again. Fin was risking a lot just keeping him here and yet still, Morgan's heart ached thinking of going back to the priory. Even if it'd be easier for all involved. He picked at a loose thread in the tablecloth, trying to distract himself.

"Did—" He swallowed, a lump in his throat, and he couldn't look up even when Fin and Eryn faced him. It made his heart beat too fast. "Did your grandmother's funeral go well?"

In Blackburn, the Divine presided over burials and they were always quiet affairs; the most Morgan ever did was say a prayer for the dead and sprinkle chrysanthemum petals into the grave plot. In larger cities like Rosenburg, it was typically delegated to trusted clergy while the Divine only visited a few. Because Morgan was in solitude, however, it wasn't like he would have attended anyway. If Fin hadn't fallen through his roof, he never would have seen Beatrice again. Pieces of her soul would have been stuck in her body.

He hardly even knew her, but it made his stomach sink.

Fin shrugged. "It was fine. Clergy as stuffy as ever."

"I don't think the prior was happy with the flower crown I made her," Eryn said as she took a loose petal from the bouquet on the table. "I'm just glad he didn't touch it."

"He saw you glaring at him every time he tried."

Morgan tried not to smile. At Beatrice with her flower crown or at the Head Prior hesitating taking it away just because Eryn was glaring at him—he wasn't sure which.

"A lot of people showed up," Eryn continued wistfully and she rested her chin on her palms. "It was really sweet. Your grandma touched a lot of people here."

"Yeah, just not my dad apparently."

That soured the warmth Morgan felt blooming in his chest at all the people seeing Beatrice off. The kettle whistled and as Fin faced it, Eryn gave Morgan an apologetic look.

The silence only remained until Fin had the table set. Plate of eggs and toast for each of them, a teacup beside each plate, and once he was sitting, they all dug in. Eryn dumped copious spoonfuls of sugar in her tea, but Morgan took his as it was and sipped on it. The orange blossom taste reminded him of the softness of the house last night. How quiet everything had been. How completely at peace he'd been. He quickly set it down, shaking the dreaminess from his thoughts, and both Fin and Eryn looked at him when the cup clinked.

He cleared his throat. "What are you going to do now with your grandmother gone?" Morgan hated how it sounded aloud and winced, but Fin didn't seem to mind. His face softened and he leaned back in his chair, thinking.

"It's the end of summer," he said. "Usually, me and Eryn head up to the beach about now."

Eryn's eyes lit up. "There's always this small gathering. Not really publicly advertised, but we happened across it once and made it a point to go back. So, it's been our thing." She spread her eggs across her toast and folded them together. "There's this bonfire, marshmallows, swimming, dancing—the works. And you can even see the fireworks Rosenburg shoots off right from the beach." She sighed and took a bite of her egg-toast. "I honestly didn't think we'd get to go this year, given... you know."

"My grandmother always went too," Fin said, staring distantly into his half-eaten eggs. The ghost of a smile spread across his lips. "She'd always watch us swim while she stayed dry in her summer dress and her huge hat. There're some paintings of that beach up in the attic. Maybe I should hang them up."

Eryn watched Fin so softly and it was with such fondness, Morgan felt bad for staring at it so long, memorizing how it looked to gaze at someone so.

"I think she'd want you to go," Eryn said. "I'm leaving for university in a few weeks. It'll be our last chance for a while. Maybe we can even stop at the fair too. We haven't been in such a long time."

The kitchen went quiet. Morgan wished he

wasn't present for the conversation; it didn't feel like one he should have been part of. He returned to his food, eating it numbly, and eventually, Fin set his fork down.

"Yeah." He nodded and met Morgan's gaze so suddenly, Morgan's heart fluttered. "You wanna come too?"

Morgan dropped his gaze back to his teacup, stammering on his words. It was a joke. He barely knew them. Inviting himself to something they shared felt wrong. He put the teacup to his lips and swallowed a mouthful before he gathered something to say.

"Are you two..." He glanced at them, lifting his eyebrows. "Together?"

Fin snorted into his tea, then coughed, practically spewing it in front of him, and Eryn laughed, slapping the table.

"No!" she said once her laughter subsided. She wiped her cheeks and made a face at Fin. He made one back before he reached behind him for a towel to wipe the spilled tea. "No. We've just been friends since Fin's dad dumped him here. We're not compatible, believe me."

"Oh." Morgan's cheeks flushed. He busied him-self with picking apart his toast. "Sorry. I've just never seen two people look so fondly at one another."

A soft sigh escaped Eryn; she'd leaned her chin back on her palm and watched him. "I guess I can see that if they never let you leave the priory much," she said. "They're just too stuffy to look at *anything* fondly, even the Lady I bet."

Morgan knew it was a joke, but he couldn't muster up a laugh. Most of the clergy was kind, but tired. Like the world rested on them when it didn't. There was so much to do in the background for Blackburn, they simply didn't have time to look at one another fondly. No one had ever been overtly warm to him in the priory. He was the Divine. Above it all.

"Were you serious?" Morgan peered at Fin. "Can I really go with you?" When Fin's face shifted, something sad overcoming it, Morgan's entire body buzzed with worry that he'd say no. "Please? I don't want to go back to the priory. I want to be me. I want to make my own memories." His heart was speeding too fast, pushing his pulse into his ears, and he couldn't keep his voice level.

They were going to say no. Even he knew it was such a selfish thing to expect. Once the priory learned he was gone, there would be panic. Fin and Eryn would get in trouble for kidnapping the Divine; no one would believe he would have gone willingly no matter what he said. It was only a matter of time before *someone* noticed the glaring hole in the spire's roof. Maybe even before his solitude was over.

Except the thought of going back terrified him more than being caught.

"Please?" he said again. "I want to be Morgan. Not the Divine."

Fin and Eryn shared a look. Morgan couldn't read the conversation they had therein, but when Fin faced him again, he was smiling. Morgan could have melted.

"I invited you," he teased. "I meant it." He leaned forward on the table and glanced Morgan up and down. "There are a few logistics, though."

"Your hair," Eryn said before Morgan could ask what. Right. Morgan was too young to have naturally white hair and it was frowned upon for young people to bleach their hair white. "Your eyes are easy. I got sunglasses." She tapped her fingers on her chin. "You also need something to wear. Something tells me you didn't come here in something *normal*."

Morgan shook his head. "Just what I wear under my robes."

Eryn nodded slowly and slid a glance at Fin. "Can't believe you even found him something to sleep in." She stood and stacked her cup and plate together. "My brother's off at boarding school—I think he's your size. I'll grab a few things and be back." She reached forward and ruffled her fingers through Morgan's hair. He stopped, frozen altogether, and she retrieved her hand. "I got ideas for your hair." She faced Fin. "Got your grandma's car gassed up still?"

Fin nodded. "It's good."

Eryn gave him a thumbs up. "I'll be back! Maybe we can make tracks before it gets too late."

She was out the door without another word, humming, and Fin stood.

"I think she's just excited for trouble." Fin reached across the table for her plate and stacked it with his. "Except she always gets *out* of trouble. I'm always left in it."

Morgan lifted his eyebrows, smiling. "Oh? Am I trouble?"

Fin winced and Morgan let himself snicker. "No, no. You're fine." Fin chuckled when he noticed Morgan smiling. He took Morgan's empty plate and cup and placed everything in the sink. "Besides, what are they gonna do if they catch me with you? They already banned me from the priory."

"They banned you?" Fired was one thing, but to keep someone from coming at all was odd. "Why?" The question left Morgan's throat before he could consider if it was a touchy question. An answer itched inside his thoughts, like he'd known why at some point, but it was so far away. Except, he couldn't have known; he'd never met Fin before last night.

The question left Fin's shoulders tense. He'd already turned on the sink, letting the water wash over the dishes, but he wouldn't look at Morgan.

So, it was touchy then. Morgan stood and came closer. "You don't have to tell me," he amended and Fin released a breath. Morgan leaned against the counter and watched Fin wash the meager plates and cups they'd used. It was probably some small slight the Head Prior blew out of proportion.

"I don't know how to swim," Morgan said instead.

Fin relaxed, smiling at him again. "We can teach you," he said. "It's about a full day's ride out—we go the long way around Rosenburg for the sights. Don't want to get stuck in there during rush hour. There's this place we usually spend the night on the way, but right before it is this field of sunflowers." He gently ran the washcloth over the teacups. "You'll like it."

Sunflowers. There was a memory associated with them, making Morgan smile and though it was small and quiet, it lit up something in his brain. He remembered a crown of soft, golden petals across his hair. It stood stark against his once black strands. Someone was smiling at him, the face long gone to the haze of memory.

He gently touched his hair, expecting the flowers to be there.

They weren't.

He must have grown too silent; Fin had stopped washing and he was watching him sadly. Before Morgan could brush it away, Fin gently nudged him with his elbow. A small laugh left Morgan's throat, a sensation too familiar from someone he didn't know beyond last night, and he nudged Fin back.

"Eryn's a touchy-feely kind of gal," Fin said. "If it bugs you, let me know. I'll tell her."

"No, it's fine," Morgan said. "It was... nice." He glanced into the sink. Just so he didn't have to look at Fin. "Do you know what happens to the parents of the Divine?"

The room stilled with the simple question and it didn't move again until Fin shook his head. "I don't," he said. "Usually Divines are older, right? Parents aren't in the equation as much."

"According to the priory books, the youngest recorded Divine before me was in her twenties." Morgan gingerly reached into the sink and retrieved one of the cups. He took the towel from Fin and gently dried it. "I suppose I'm now the youngest recorded Divine."

"Do you want to find your parents? Do you think

they still live here?"

Morgan shrugged. "I wouldn't even recognize them. Maybe they wouldn't even recognize me. I don't know if I want to put them through that. Not being remembered." He let Beatrice's memory guide him and opened the correct cupboard to place the dry cup home before reaching for another one. "I wish I knew them, but it's fleeting. It's not like they'd know me anymore. We're strangers."

Maybe it was something too morose to say. Fin didn't reply. He simply continued washing the dishes and Morgan rinsed them before he dried. A quiet routine. When they finished, Fin dried the counter down and Morgan watched as the water and soap swirled down the drain.

"Hey... Morgan?" Fin whispered and Morgan looked at him. Fin's shoulders were tense again, but he hadn't faced Morgan.

The door opened before he said any more and Fin dropped whatever it was to launch himself in front of Morgan. It was only Eryn; she skipped inside without a care in the world, having changed into a pair of high-waisted shorts, sneakers, and a buttoned-up shirt tied in the front. Hanging off her arm was a flower printed tote bag.

Fin released a sigh and stepped away from Morgan.

"All yours," Fin said and although Morgan wanted to press him on what he'd been saying, he remained quiet instead. Must not have mattered. "I'll get changed and find us something to eat on the way."

Eryn wasted no time once Fin was gone; she found Morgan a stool, shuffled him onto it, and had Morgan's head under the sink nozzle. At least the water was already warmed, but Morgan still flinched as it hit the nape of his neck. Once the initial shock was over, the water was soothing as it cascaded through his hair, especially when Eryn gently ran her fingers through it. The sensation reminded Morgan of when he was younger—or at least, he hoped it was his memory. Whosever's it was, it was simply peace. Gentle fingers washing his hair, humming a tune soft against the rush of water, and Morgan dragged himself back to reality.

Eryn wasn't humming. She hadn't even started talking again. She was fussing with something in her tote bag. Morgan cleared his throat, hoping to get her talking so he could stay here and not steeped in some memory that wasn't his.

"D-Do you work in Blackburn?"

"Yeah! I'm too loud for the priory." Eryn set a small bottle beside the sink. "Head down, this is a wash-in dye. It'll last for a few days." When Morgan ducked his head, Eryn uncapped the bottle. "My aunt is the director at the library and since I always helped out when I wasn't busy, she let me apprentice under her in my gap year."

"Gap year?" Morgan asked.

"Higher education in these parts like to encourage graduates to learn something about the field they want to go in before heading off to a university," Eryn explained. "So, most of us get a gap year between high school and university. I knew what I wanted to do right away... Fin? Not so much."

Morgan frowned. "Why not?"

Eryn shrugged. "The whole priory thing didn't stick and then his grandmother got really sick. He's behind, but it'll be fine now. I'm sure of it." She indicated the sink again and Morgan laid his head back down in it. She took a stirrer from the drawer and stuck it into the bottle to swirl the contents. "I keep trying to say he should just find something to do at the library. I like it and it'd be nice to go away to school together for library things."

"What do you do at the library?" Morgan asked.

"I usually help out with the kids. They'll think I'm cool until they grow up." She sighed wistfully. "I'll miss this place while I'm gone. Cities are so large and loud."

Rosenburg certainly fit the description; large

and loud, but impossibly alive at the same time. It hardly felt as simple as Blackburn.

Eryn upturned the bottle and squeezed it. Whatever came out was a goopy black and smelled awful. As she threaded her fingers through his hair, spreading the dye, Morgan couldn't help but scrunch his nose. The gesture was not lost on Eryn and she laughed.

"Yeah, it smells *bad*." She smoothed it through his hair with gentle motions. "I used it for this play these kids were doing for school. I hated it then too." She withdrew her hands and took another moment before she spoke. "This is *not* soaking in like it should."

Morgan frowned. "It's not?"

Eryn lathered harder, making Morgan wince. "Not the way it needs to. Your hair should be soaking it in—it's *white*. Has no color. I've helped old ladies dye their hair the same way and it *always* soaks right in." She huffed and ran the water over his head. Black ribbons spooled into the sink below, staining it in a swirl of black.

"What's wrong?" Fin asked from behind the gentle wash of water.

Eryn stopped scrubbing Morgan's hair and threw a towel over his head.

"Dye isn't sticking," she said.

Morgan ran the towel through his hair, expecting them to change their mind, but when he pulled the towel away from his face, he found Fin in front of him. Too close. Heat crept up his neck as Fin gently checked his head. After a moment, he shrugged and stepped back.

"Guess the white hair really is something mystical," he said. "We have hats."

He'd changed into something casual; a layered white and black tank top paired with black trousers rolled up at the ankles. Even his shoes were already on—the same scruffy sneakers he'd worn on their flight from the priory.

As Morgan tore his gaze away, trying not to think about Fin entirely and focus on drying his hair instead, Fin turned and examined the small pile of folded clothes in Eryn's tote bag. He checked them one by one, nodding, and glanced at Morgan and then back at Eryn with an expression Morgan couldn't quite read.

"Hey, Eryn?" he said. She stopped fussing with wiping her hands and raised her eyebrows. "Felicity still at the library?"

Eryn tilted her head. "Yeah, though I don't work with her a lot since she's part of the morning crew. Why?"

"Didn't she used to work at the priory?"

Felicity. Morgan repeated the name to himself as he folded the towel. Sparks of familiarity tinged it and he watched Eryn, hopeful. She appeared thoughtful, tapping a finger on her chin.

"She mentioned it when she applied," she said. "They gave her a glowing recommendation too." She noticed Morgan looking at her and gave him a weak smile. "Wait, what? Did you know her?"

"I had a friend," Morgan said quickly. "S-She'd bring me old library books."

Eryn's face brightened. "I wonder if it *is* her! She always came by when she worked at the priory looking for books we'd withdrawn. I never knew what she was doing with them and she never told us even when we hired her." She framed her fingers over her eyes like glasses. "Thick glasses, bushy black hair? Freckles?"

More and more, a picture of her tried to slot itself together in his mind. Glasses and freckles. Hair escaping its confines. Morgan eagerly nodded. "It sounds like her."

Fin grinned. "Want to make a pit stop before we leave Blackburn? I bet she's at the library today."

"Yes," Morgan breathed without even thinking it through. "Yes." He nodded and took the set of folded clothes Fin pulled free for him. "You'd really take me?"

"Of course," Fin said. "Come on, get dressed. We can make it before it gets too busy."

New adventures all the time. More than just leaving Blackburn of his own accord; he was seeing someone the clergy had taken away from him. He could have practically skipped to the bathroom thinking about what he wanted to say to Felicity—if it even was her. But it had to be. The name was so familiar.

He knew there was a real smile on his lips and he didn't care how goofy it was as he headed through the hall. He didn't even mind his reflection in the mirror this time.

All he saw was Morgan smiling at him. Not the Divine. Not someone he fought to remember each morning, but himself.

VII.
FRIEND IN THE BOOKS

Even in someone else's clothes, Morgan felt more and more like something he'd call himself. The clothes weren't anything special, just a plain tank top beneath Fin's hooded jacket (and Morgan took a selfish moment to wrap it tight around himself to breathe it in deep), black shorts that fell past his knees, socks and sneakers, and a snug newsboy cap to hide his hair. People would still be able to see his white hair if they cared to look, but Eryn was confident the chances of someone doing so were pretty small. The only thing Morgan kept from his old outfit was the cord of red around his waist. For some reason, he just couldn't leave it behind.

All in all, he looked normal. It was nice.

Fin and Eryn had been busy while Morgan

washed and changed; Fin had haphazardly slapped sandwiches together, wrapped them in wax paper, and had them inside the cooler now sitting on the table. Eryn had chopped some fruit from the refrigerator and threw it in too. A few bottles of water were last to go in and then the cooler was clasped shut. Eryn had three tote bags packed full of a change of clothes, bathing suits, toiletries for the three of them, and one had Fin's instant camera safely nestled inside. Everything needed for a short road trip.

Fin lugged the cooler through the door, and Eryn and Morgan followed with the totes.

The car had been backed out and idled in front of the house. Morgan couldn't really say what kind of car it was, just that it was old. A dusty white, it had two doors, and the bumper was askew on the back. Definitely not nearly as maintained as the cab from the Rosenburg Priory, but at the same time, lived in. Real. There was a beaded necklace hanging from the review mirror, the gems yellow and orange, and at the end was a ceramic fake sunflower.

Before they reached the car, Eryn stopped like a thought occurred to her and beamed at Fin. "We should take a photo in front of the house," she said and nudged Morgan. "More memories, right?"

He nodded eagerly and turned to Fin. "Can all three of us get in the shot?"

Fin thought for a moment before he settled the cooler on the hood of the car, grinning. "I'm game to try."

Morgan ended up sandwiched between Fin and Eryn as they held the camera between themselves. On one hand, it was nice. Like real friends. Not just people dealing with him. On the other, Morgan's entire body felt like it was on fire being so close to another person as it took ages for the camera to take the shot. Still, Morgan couldn't hide his joy as he gazed at the new photo. His smile was awkward, his shoulders tense, but he was beginning to recognize himself.

Not as the Divine, but as Morgan.

"Thank you," Morgan found himself saying quietly after they'd all seen the photo. It went with the others, his growing collection. Memories to take back with him to the priory.

If he even wanted to go back.

No. Thinking of it would just undo everything good he'd felt the entire day. He had to stop and live in the present. What came tomorrow or the next day didn't matter. Morgan brushed it away the best he could and watched as Fin and Eryn loaded the car.

The passenger seat had been pushed forward and after a bit of twisting and squeezing, Fin and Eryn got the cooler in the backseat and buckled it in.

The totes were settled beside it on the floor and Fin popped the seat back into position. Eryn slid inside immediately, positioning herself dead center, and when Morgan didn't follow, she peeked out and patted the seat beside her.

"Come on, there's room!" she said. "I'm used to sitting in the middle."

Morgan gingerly slipped in and breathed out. He'd never actually sat in a vehicle other than a priory cab before. It was weird. Eryn reached over him to shut the passenger door and his cheeks flared with embarrassment forgetting something so basic. Fin lingered outside for another moment, eyes cast on the house, but before either Morgan or Eryn could ask if something was wrong, he slid into the driver's side and shut his door.

Enclosed, the car smelled like Fin's house, but also like a certain perfume reminiscent of flowers. Somehow, deep down, Morgan knew it was Beatrice. Her memories trickled to the surface, but they made Morgan smile this time. Maybe part of her would always linger in the places she'd called home and ready to greet him like a friend. For once, he didn't think he'd mind.

Fin maneuvered through the snaking road, taking them past the old houses sleepily coming alive as their tenants began their day. Morgan couldn't deny his excitement, but the closer they came to the library, the more doubt crawled across it. He wanted to say it was because they were traveling down the main street and he could easily be seen, but that wasn't right. It was Felicity herself.

He'd agreed to see her. The name still lit a memory buried deep beyond all the other ones. Shaking her hand. How warm it had been and how unlike the others, she wasn't hurrying to let go. Then there were the mornings she greeted him with her latest theory of one of the books she'd given him to read. Or how what her book club thought about it was wrong. All those nights he stayed up late reading, thinking of what to say so he could theorize with her. She'd done so much so he could have a friend in the silent halls of the priory.

He wanted so badly to meet her again as Morgan, not the Divine; wanted to see her again as Felicity, not his attendant. But what if the warmth and friendship had just been part of her job? What if she blamed *him* for losing her job? The thoughts opened a hole in his stomach, letting all the what ifs linger and blossom into more doubts. It made him numb, even as they stopped in front of the library. He hardly noticed himself getting out of the car, Eryn right behind him, and hardly registered her leaving them in the alley so she could she hurry inside the side door. It was only when she already done did reality catch up and Morgan thought to change his mind.

The library was small, the alley tight between it and the building next door. Morgan had no idea what the other building was, but it had no windows facing them. He was safe here away from prying eyes. Ivy clung to the side of the library, growing along a patch of grass between it and the road, and practically covered it if not for someone's well-meaning attempt to trim it back. The side door had been propped open with a wooden wedge, letting the summer breeze inside, and Fin had taken Morgan to wait beside it amidst the small wildflowers growing at their feet.

"Hey," Fin whispered, eyebrows drawn together in concern. "Are you okay? You're shaking."

Morgan swallowed, trying to stop. He couldn't say no—not now since they were already here. He tensed as Fin slid closer and gently rubbed his back. It was a warm, loving gesture, and Morgan's tension slowly eased out of him.

"I can grab Eryn if you've changed your mind," Fin said. "We don't have to do this if it's too much."

Before Morgan could decide if it *was* too much, force an answer from his throat, he heard Eryn's voice near the door. He tensed back up, straining his ears to listen, and became all too aware of how loud his heart was thumping in his chest.

"I just have a question, Felicity! Don't give me that look," Eryn said from inside, her voice teasing. "The stacks will be there when you come back. I promise."

"Honestly—it's your day off," came Felicity's voice—and Morgan knew it was her without a doubt even if she herself was a fuzzy image. Her voice sung true through his memory.

"I don't know why you couldn't just ask me while I worked," Felicity continued.

"Private question!" Eryn said. "You worked at the priory." Not a question. A fact.

"Yes, and you *know* that already." Felicity paused, suspicion in her voice. "Did something happen at Mrs. Thorne's funeral? I'm so sorry I couldn't go. I just felt awkward since I didn't know Fin or her well and—I guess—"

"No, no, it was fine as far as funerals go," Eryn cut her off. "You were the Divine's attendant, right?"

The sudden silence became poignant in an instant. Fin's hand had stopped rubbing Morgan's back, but he also hadn't stopped watching Morgan. Giving him an out when honestly, Morgan shouldn't have needed one. It shouldn't have been so hard to imagine saying hi to Felicity—an old friend. If she even was one.

"Who told you that?" Felicity broke the silence and her voice came quick and sharp. "I never told anyone here. Your aunt doesn't even know."

"I just wanted to know for sure!" Eryn said. "You see—"

"Wait." Felicity gasped. "Is he... is he—"

Morgan's heart hadn't stopped beating so fast. He was dizzy. Sick. No. He couldn't do this. Memories were all she was; he'd ruined whatever life she had at the priory by letting her be friendly. He should have rejected all of the books, put mental walls between himself and her, and never hoped for anything more. It was always bound to be ruined.

He couldn't ruin the little memories he had just in case something went horribly wrong seeing her again or she turned him in. Before he could grip Fin's hand—tell him he wanted to go back—a woman in a gray dress rushed out of the doorway despite Eryn's attempt to stop her.

She halted in front of Morgan and her jaw dropped. She had the same brown skin splashed with freckles she had before, the same bushy black hair framing her face, and the same black glasses set upon her nose.

It really *was* Felicity.

They were frozen for a single stunned moment,

like she became acutely aware that yes, he was Morgan—the Divine—standing in front of her without his veil and robes. The moment broke when she lurched forward and tightly wrapped her arms around him in a crushing hug. She held him so tightly, like she was afraid if she let go, he simply wouldn't be there. He'd forgotten how tall she was and how she always smelled like jasmine and lavender.

"Hey, Felicity?" Eryn's voice ruptured the warm silence. "Please don't crush him. Clergy might notice."

A laugh bubbled out of Felicity, one so infectious, Morgan started laughing too, and she pulled away. Her hands never left his shoulders, though, as she looked him over in a way she never would have been allowed to at the priory. He wiped his cheeks, eyes suddenly brimming with tears, and he tried smiling at her. She returned it, reminding him of the many he'd seen before.

"I've wanted to do that for such a long time," Felicity said. "Especially when they asked me to resign." She let him go, hands trembling. "All because I wanted to be your friend. Not just your attendant." She took her glasses off and wiped them on her blouse. Fidgeting so she didn't have to look at Morgan directly.

Not that he minded with how he struggled to find his voice. It was trapped behind a lump in his throat. "I—I..." He swallowed and breathed in. "I wanted to be your friend too," he whispered. "I'm sorry I messed it up."

Felicity slid her glasses back into place and shook her head. "It was never you. It was always Head Prior Augustus," she said. "You were simply you." She took in a breath and put a scrutinizing eye on Fin over Morgan's shoulder. Her lips parted into a teasing grin. "This is your doing, isn't it?"

Fin balked, palming his chest. "Hey! Why do you think it was me?" He immediately bit back a laugh, like it was obvious why.

"The old ladies are always saying what a trouble-maker you are with that face," Felicity said. Fin let out an exaggerated sigh in lieu of an answer, dropping his shoulders, and Morgan had to smother his own laugh. Felicity faced Eryn beside her. "Where are you taking him? Not just to see me, I assume."

"Up to the beach for the bonfire," Eryn said. "Clergy won't even realize he's gone."

Felicity's smile softened as she faced Morgan again. "I wish I could go with." Her hands twitched with hesitation before she pulled him into another hug. Still as warm as the first, but not quite as crushing. Morgan leaned into it, hugging her back, and they separated shortly. She took a deep breath and nodded.

"Stop by again before you head back to the priory," she said. "I'll make a care package of books."

Before he headed back. Because the reality was that he'd have to, at some point. He managed another smile anyway, nodding because his voice refused to work. This time, he'd keep the books. Even if the clergy eventually found them, he'd keep them for as long as he could. He'd remember her face, all of its gentle curves, how sharp her brown eyes were, and how she was as Felicity, not as his attendant. He wouldn't forget.

He promised himself.

They were back on the road shortly, the sun shining down on them as they went. Blackburn had woken up entirely, the streets teeming with life simply going on. No one stole a glance at Fin's car as they drove away from the library and Morgan watched as Blackburn slid past them. It wasn't like he had reason to hide; no one knew the Divine had left the priory of his own accord, much less that he'd be riding in Fin's car.

And they'd never know.

Eryn righted herself in her seat after fishing out a bag of apple slices. She handed a wedge to Morgan, smiling. "I'm glad you got to see Felicity."

He was too and nodded as he gently nibbled on his piece.

"We'll definitely bring you by again," Fin added as he casually steered his way through Blackburn's main street. "I'm sure I can carry you *and* a bag of books up." He winked at Morgan, smiling.

Morgan's face flushed. "I'd like that," he said quietly.

Blackburn thinned out soon enough, buildings giving way to fields in either direction and a clear road lay ahead of them. The summer air whistled by the open windows and Morgan settled against the seat.

He was leaving. Officially of his own accord. And, even though he knew the thought should have terrified him because of what it meant, he never wanted to return.

VIII.
SUNFLOWERS

Fin had a lazy confidence as he drove; once they'd reached a constant speed, he kept one hand on the wheel and propped his other arm on the driver side window. Helpfully, there weren't many cars on the road alongside them and it let Fin set a more leisurely pace.

Soft music played from the radio, and Eryn made sure it *stayed* music. She never let it linger long on an advertisement or talk show and if it did, she popped out a cassette from the glovebox and threw it in. Morgan hadn't listened to music often beyond what the priory organist played during sermons; this was a great deal more unique and Morgan liked it. Maybe music would have helped the long bouts of silence in solitude if the priory had just let him have it. Maybe he should have asked.

Eryn tired of staying quiet soon into the drive and told Morgan all about the library. It had recently ended its summer program that helped encourage kids to read. Apparently, she mostly headed the crafts and recalled once going home trailing untold amounts of glitter after her. It was easy conversation. Superficial. Filtered in one ear and out the window to join the summer air.

Well into their drive, they parked at a small rest stop off the main road so Eryn and Fin could both stretch their legs and go for a bathroom break. Morgan stayed in the car, keeping the hood and hat over his head. He hadn't been chugging water like they'd been, so he really didn't need to go, and he was too scared to risk getting out.

Although on second thought, the parking lot was pretty empty. He probably would have been fine. Besides Fin's car, there was only a motorcycle parked down at the end of the lane. No one by the motor-cycle, but it had two helmets hanging from the handlebars. He found himself strangely drawn to the bike; he hadn't seen them often, only a few times when he'd been taken out to Rosenburg. They were always noisy and he hated hearing them while he was trapped in the cab, but without the noise and without the discomfort of a priory cab, it was actually rather sleek.

Maybe it would have been nice to go for a ride, just feeling the wind completely blow through his body. Like the pedal bike, but probably more. He was stuck in the daydream, wondering how it would really feel, when Fin and Eryn came back. Fin caught Morgan looking at the bike as he slipped out to let Eryn back into her center seat, and snickered.

"If only I had one of those. Lot faster than my pedal bike," Fin said. "That'd be a lot of fun, right?" He grinned wide and butterflies stirred in Morgan's stomach. "Just us and the road."

"Hey!" Eryn poked her head out. "Then you wouldn't have brought me!" She giggled as Fin gave her an exasperated sigh and slipped back inside. "Come on, let's get going! Wasting daylight!"

They returned to the easy chatter as they drove, wind whipping by the windows, and Morgan settled into his new normal. It was so much more than riding in a priory cab. There, his every movement was watched to make sure he was *fine*. Even when they didn't truly care about him. Just if he could do what was asked of the Divine. That was all that mattered in the end.

Morgan hated that he kept dwelling. He wanted to focus on the moment. Focus on his new friends. Think of how much they could do together without the worry of the clergy deeming it inappropriate and splitting them up.

The very thought made goosebumps flush down his arms.

No. They wouldn't do it this time. He wouldn't allow them to.

Fin split off from the traffic heading toward Rosenburg and they headed down into a concrete tunnel, jolting Morgan back to reality. It stole away the summer air, washing the smell of concrete and asphalt into the car instead. The radio fuzzed with static and though Eryn attempted to rectify it, she gave up and threw in another cassette. The song broken with static had its own kind of charm, and Morgan missed it. Not enough to complain and he busied himself with watching the lights go by along the tunnel walls. Just as his eyelids drooped, his body begging for a quick nap, Eryn jostled his shoulder.

"Don't fall asleep! Watch—we're almost at the end!"

Late afternoon sunlight showered the end of the tunnel, making it a bright white, and grew closer with every second. Beyond the smell of the industrial concrete, Morgan finally caught something else. Flowers. As the car slipped out of the tunnel, the light was too bright and Morgan had to squint.

When his eyes readjusted, there was a slope of

pine trees to one side where the sun was setting behind them, and on the other against a backdrop of rolling hills was a field of sunflowers. There were so many of them, each a golden blaze of yellow turned toward the sky. It looked almost like a fantasy and Morgan wanted to reach out to touch them, make sure they were real, but he feared asking to stop. Instead, he made due with watching them so he'd never forget. He folded his arms on the window, rested his head against them, and even breathed in deep to fill his lungs with sunflowers so he'd never forget.

"We tried growing a sunflower once," Eryn said and Fin snorted beside her. "It did not get nearly as big."

"I'm pretty sure it *died*," Fin said. "Didn't even get a chance."

"We were twelve! We did our best!"

A muffled sob broke through their voices. Morgan jerked up, eyes wide. His skin tingled, a brush of broken memories touching it, but then it was gone. Goosebumps raced across his entire body and he stuck his head out the window, ignoring Eryn's and Fin's shout of surprise. The hat went flying, but he didn't care even as his hair whipped in the wind. The sob came from the receding sunflowers. Eryn tugged at him, yelling, but her voice was so far away.

Someone was crying. The sunflowers swayed gently in the wind, no sign that anyone was there, and when Morgan blinked, the world slowed. Petals glistened below the evening sunlight with an other-worldly gleam. Then Morgan felt a little hand reach into him and tug. Something was there. He couldn't ignore it. He had to get closer.

He let Eryn pull him inside, the world rushing back to normal speed, and she clattered into her seat with a huff.

"Stop," Morgan cut Eryn off and she snapped her mouth shut. "Fin, stop the car."

Fin immediately ceased whatever it was he'd been attempting to say about the hat.

"*Please*," Morgan said. "Stop the car."

Fin did, though he had his mouth open with a question. As soon as Morgan deemed it safe, he freed himself from the seatbelt and threw the door open. Eryn shouted something, the car jerked to a complete stop, and Morgan nearly tripped as he stepped onto the road. None of it mattered. Only the crying did.

"What's wrong?" Fin asked as he slipped out of the driver's side.

The wind carried the voice toward them, but it remained so distant and faint. Like it was hardly there at all.

"I hear crying," Morgan whispered. He strained his ears to listen. It had to be in the sunflowers.

He was aware of the look Fin and Eryn shared over the top of the car. Aware they couldn't hear it themselves. The crying wasn't alive; it was barely holding on as it was, begging for *someone* to listen. And Morgan would.

His legs were already running before he'd fully decided. Fin and Eryn shouted after him, but their voices were ripples through a haze of dreams as he concentrated so hard on the voice begging for help. The car doors slamming sounded the same, but Morgan had to focus. He needed to find the source of the crying. Everything else could come later and he plunged himself into the throng of sunflower stalks.

"Morgan! Wait!" Fin called, his voice cutting through clearly, but Morgan ignored it.

It wasn't their fault they couldn't hear it. Couldn't understand. The dead sung only for the Divine. Sometimes it was lyrical and full of the life they lived, like Beatrice's. Other times it was a surge of panic, like those who died in the fire. This one, however, was lonely and sad. Barely a whimper. On the verge of breaking entirely. He couldn't wait.

Morgan didn't know exactly how far he'd run;

his legs and lungs burned, but it didn't truly feel long before he escaped the wall of sunflowers and found the smallest clearing between them. His heart lurched into his throat when he saw it: the small body lying on the ground, decomposing. It was so small, so thin. Barely even a life lived.

Fin and Eryn ran into his back, nearly throwing him forward, but Fin caught him around his shoulders. Morgan was glad; he might have collapsed otherwise. The smell hit them harder than it had Morgan; Eryn immediately retreated, vomiting into the patch of grass behind them, and Fin released Morgan, coughing, and covered his mouth and nose.

However strong the smell was, Morgan couldn't let it bother him. Not when Divines long before him had to deal with the dead without herbs to mask it.

Morgan stepped forward until Fin latched an arm around his chest and wrenched him back.

"Let me go." Morgan pulled himself away and glared at Fin and Eryn, but they only responded with their own worried looks. "You don't have to come near." He faced the small body again, swallowing. "I have to do this."

Because if no one did soon, the soul would truly die.

Trembling, Morgan knelt beside the body. Truth be told, he wanted to vomit like Eryn. His heart raced. His pulse buzzed. He thought it might happen as his breathing turned ragged and sharp, but he managed to keep it together.

Carefully, he touched the body's cheek, what remained of it, and the soul flickered. It flitted across his fingers, slipping and struggling. It was barely holding on as it was.

"H-How long—" Eryn said between gasping breaths. "H-How long has this been here?"

"I don't know," Morgan whispered, irritation trickling into his voice. "Please, be quiet." What he wouldn't give for the solitary sending room of the priory. Even the morgue was better than their panicked breathing mixed with the crickets singing around them.

He bent low, bringing his lips as close as he could, and the soul leapt at him, no coaxing needed. It traced its little fingers across his face, pressing down on his eyes, and against his lips. Goosebumps flew across Morgan's entire body at how cold the touch felt; those from the fire had invited warmth of one kind and Beatrice had brought another kind. This was like it would frost Morgan's skin before long, but he had to endure it for the dead's sake, and invited it inside.

Memories washed over his. Broken. Fragmented. Not whole; snapshots flying by. She was crying. Screaming. Running until her legs gave out. Someone had been chasing her, but she'd lost them when she'd thrown herself into the field. Her legs became weak, her lungs struggling to keep up, and she came to a stop here. She'd bled too much to move any longer. No one heard her pleas for help. Her final memory, the only one clear, was the last thing she ever saw: the stars twinkling above her as her body gave out. She'd counted them as high as she could, her heart slowing with each raspy breath, and then there was spiraling darkness.

It gripped Morgan hard and fast, like fingers digging into his arms attempting to take him down too, and he opened his eyes. Darkness. No. Too deep. He ripped his arms up and the memory released him, letting him see again. Dark, purple bruises bloomed across his arms. Little red scratches dug deep from nails desperate to hold on. The pain burrowed, making him tremble, and Morgan took in a deep breath to ground himself. She was desperate and scared. It wasn't unheard of for some physical manifestation to happen when the Divine interacted with souls, but it wasn't often because Divines were supposed to be prompt, arriving well before the soul's desperation kicked in. It didn't help it was a little girl who likely didn't understand sendings like adults did.

As Morgan grounded himself in reality—felt the late summer breeze wash over his clammy skin—he noticed her blood around them. It had stained deep into the ground, its red hue lost to a dark brown.

Morgan sucked in another deep breath and focused. The girl's soul was still stubbornly attached to her remains. She must have known she was dead, but her body was all she'd ever known. She was still scared. All he'd done was make her relive her terrifying last hours. For all she knew, he could have been the one who'd harmed her. He needed to reach further.

He exhaled, calming his racing heart, and bent close once more.

Children were different than adults; they clung to the life still rightfully theirs, even if it had long since given them up. Adults generally came to terms with their deaths because on some level, they understood the concept. Children didn't.

Without another idea, he hummed to her, something soft and slow reminiscent of the hymn deep in everyone's memories. It wasn't long before her crying wail ceased, rebuilding her voice into a soft timbre to match his and she hummed with him. Though it started broken, struggling to form another sound that wasn't a cry, it slowly began to even and a little hand slid into his. Morgan held it delicately between his fingers and the soul came to him a second time.

Softer memories bloomed, those in which a child would cherish. Petting a dog as it tried just as hard to pet her little hand back. Curling up against her mother as she read a tale of brave princesses. Holding her parents' hands as they strolled through a forest road, the sun streaming down around them. Eating cake with more frosting than cake while smiling at everyone singing to her.

Her hand squeezed tighter, little fingers looping his so desperately.

"It's okay," Morgan whispered. There was a different voice behind his. A soft rumble shivering through the air and the girl leaned into it. Another hand covered Morgan's, one with spectral skin shimmering like starlight. "You're safe now. The Lord of Night has come to protect you. The Lady of Dawn will breathe new life for you, so please. Come to me."

She threw her arms around Morgan's neck in a hug, something real and tangible, before she slid right through his body and into the spectral arms awaiting her right behind him. The Lord of Night took her into his graces, leaving Morgan shivering and empty, like always. And yet, it didn't feel like enough. All he could do was provide her grace in her death. Nothing more to stop whoever had done it.

Morgan sat back on his knees and closed his eyes. At least she left remembering her life, not her death. The joys, not what led her here, dying alone with only the stars as witness she'd been there at all.

Warmth trickled down his nose and he tasted it on his lips. A sending hadn't made his nose bleed for a long time. The first time it'd happened, the veil had been destroyed; a long streak of blood had bloomed a vibrant red through the fabric. The only saving grace was the clergy hadn't guilted him; it was common with new Divines and they had spare veils. The power simply wore on the body, especially Morgan's.

Tears trickled down his cheeks next before he could even wipe the blood.

The bloom of memories faded, leaving him completely empty. The world grew so quiet and distant around him to match. Like nothing was real.

"Morgan?"

Fin's voice broke through the emptiness and Morgan flinched, clasping his hands to his nose to stop the bleeding.

My name is Morgan, he told himself, slowly mouthing the syllables of his name. *My mother's name is Cynthia. My father left me a blanket he made.* Morgan sucked in a breath, tasting more blood. He squeezed his eyes shut, holding onto himself as the fuzziness grew. *My name is Morgan. My friends are Fin and Eryn. My name is Morgan.*

A hand settled on his shoulder and he jolted. The world returned, so close and near, so stark and real, and he flinched. Fin had knelt beside him, unwavering despite how close he was to the remains. Fin was real. He was still here. He dug out a cloth handkerchief from his pocket and pressed it into Morgan's hands.

Real. He was real.

"Is—" Eryn spoke from behind them, her voice still weak. The grass crinkled as she stepped closer. Morgan pressed the handkerchief to his nose. "Is she all right now?"

Morgan nodded, drawing a long breath through the fabric. "I gave her a sending," he said, his voice as weak as Eryn's. He finished wiping his nose and hands both. His eyes blurred with more tears and he tried to blink them back. "How did no one know she was gone?"

The question lingered in the air. Another one burned through Morgan and he faced Fin and Eryn. "How didn't anyone know she died? Why isn't anyone looking for her?"

Fin's eyebrows creased together as he frowned. "I don't think she was from Blackburn."

It shouldn't have mattered. She shouldn't have

been left here, all alone. Dying. She shouldn't have been hurt. His breathing quickened, his chest tightened, and tears streaked down his cheeks again. He didn't have enough information to help find whoever had hurt her. All Morgan could do was provide her peace in death—finality—and it *still* felt like he'd failed her.

"We're coming up to the motel soon. They'll have a phone we can use." Fin gently took Morgan's hand from his head and Morgan flinched, taking the other one away too. He hadn't realized he'd gone to grip his hair on sheer frustration alone. Fin kept hold of his hand, gently squeezing it. "I'll call my dad and tell him. He'll know who to talk to. If someone's missing, Rosenburg will send someone out."

"And if no one is?" Morgan asked, his voice cracking.

Eryn settled on his other side, rubbing her hand in circles against his back. "They'll come out any-way," she said.

She had no proof they would. There should have been more they could do. The girl had been so close to simply being gone, becoming a void in the world where she'd been. Except, despite his wants otherwise, he knew he'd done all he could.

Morgan nodded, trying to calm down, and Eryn took her hand away. She broke one of the shorter sunflower buds off and placed it beside the girl's remains.

"I wish we could wrap her up," Eryn whispered.

"We shouldn't disturb her more than we already have," Fin said. "Just in case."

The sunflower was the best they could do in lieu of any actual funeral flowers. Maybe when the city came for her, she'd get the proper funeral treatment as much as she could. Morgan only hoped so.

Morgan forced himself to stand. His legs wobbled beneath him, forgetting the strength they'd had when he was running, and Fin helped keep him upright, hand at his back. The hand brought with it a familiar sensation. The same hand once in a fuzzy memory too far gone to parse and then it abated. Déjà vu, perhaps. It didn't matter. They needed to get back to the car. It was late; the dark shroud over the sunflowers only kept at bay from the ghostly last rays of dusk in the distance.

They trudged in silence until Eryn squeaked. She hurried forward and took something off a sunflower beside them.

"Found the hat!" She gave Morgan a sad smile and secured it over his head. "There. Morgan again."

He *was* Morgan. Even if he'd just done something distinctly Divine while running away from it all. He'd wanted so badly to preserve the girl's soul because if not for him, no one would have. Marcella would have been too late had anyone actually found the body. When the city eventually came out, she'd find no soul. Perhaps she'd feel guilty, but sometimes, the soul just wasn't there. Sometimes, they were too late.

Morgan would remember her for Marcella. The girl's soul was safe.

The ensuing silence between the three of them itched into Morgan's head. It brought with it fire coating each and every sunflower, burning the petals into embers. It wasn't real; Morgan didn't bother giving life to the illusion by telling Fin and Eryn what he saw, even when he flinched as the embers touched him. Memories simply mixed together in some waking nightmare he alone had to endure.

All he wanted was return to Fin's bed and sleep it all away. Forget about the fire. Forget about a little girl dying all alone. Forget his divinity.

He wished Fin and Eryn would say something. Anything. Fill the gaps between them with noise so he could ignore the fire brushing against his skin. As it was, they stayed silent. The flames only dissipated when they left the sunflowers and spotted their lonely car on the road shoulder.

Someone else was with it.

Underneath the soft orange of the streetlight

paces away from their car was a motorcycle. One so similar to the one he'd seen at the rest stop. A woman sat on the back this time, helmet in her lap while another helmet balanced on the bike's handle. A man had approached their car.

Eryn immediately took Morgan's arm and placed him safely behind her. Fin strode forward faster, shoulders tense.

"Hey!" he called.

The woman noticed Fin first and her face brightened. She waved her hand at her partner near the car.

"Vesper!" she called out. "Vesper, come back!"

The man stopped short of peeking into their car and turned to them.

Familiarity washed over Morgan as he made eye contact with the man, and the acknowledgement made his entire body buzz. Vesper had shocking white hair in the dark with black roots close to his scalp, and it was cleverly styled to one side. He wore a white t-shirt tucked into black jeans with his sleeves rolled up, showing off star constellations tattooed across his shoulders and arms. Atop his shirt was a leather vest with a large patch of a chrysanthemum on the back while the front had stars and eyes all over. His gaze lingered too long, making the buzzing even worse, and Morgan cut his away.

Looking at the woman was no better; she was just as familiar, but instead of the overwhelming buzz, all Morgan felt from her was immense warmth. She had long, honey brown hair pulled into a fishtail braid over her shoulder and some strands gleamed gold beneath the streetlight. She wore a plain t-shirt tucked into her jeans and had the sleeves rolled up like Vesper's and her shoulders were tattooed with suns instead of constellations.

Morgan knew neither of them—he was sure—but it felt like he should have and his stomach flipped.

Eryn stood steady in front of him, clearly intent not to let him any closer, but he stepped beside her so he could listen. Eryn gave him a look, exhaling sharply through her nose, but instead of asking him why, she took his hand. She was scared; Morgan had to respect that. At the very least, they wouldn't lose each other if they ran back into the sunflowers.

"Hey." Vesper lifted his hand in greeting, his smile tilting a little more to one side than the other. His voice made Morgan shudder; he'd heard it before, but he couldn't remember exactly where. Vesper came around slowly until he stood an arm's length from Fin.

"Hey," Fin said, voice as taut as his shoulders.

"I suppose this is your car then." Vesper slid his

hands into his pockets. "Aurora got worried so we stopped to check if you were stranded."

"We're not," Fin replied.

"Funny place to stop." Aurora tilted her head and gazed around them. When no one attempted to make up a story, she tapped the helmet in her lap with her bright yellow nails. "Just checking out the sunflowers?"

Eryn cleared her voice and touched the rim of Morgan's hat, pulling it lower for him. "He just lost his hat." A weak chuckle bubbled out of her throat. "It blew right out the window."

"Ah." Vesper lifted his gaze and Morgan looked at anything else. "The wind does that."

"What are you two doing out here this late?" Fin asked, glancing toward the bike.

"Night drives are something we enjoy," Vesper said, following Fin's gaze. "It's quieter that way." He headed to his bike and took the helmet off the handle. Aurora fastened hers to her head, smiling warmly at them. "Where are you three headed anyway?"

"Just a road trip," Fin said.

Vesper nodded slowly and fastened his helmet. "Equinox is coming up. I bet you're headed to that little bonfire shindig at the beach?" He slid back on his bike just as Eryn pressed Morgan closer, like she was ready to run. "We've been there a few times. Friends with the people that organize it." Aurora wrapped her arms around Vesper's waist and he turned the ignition on the bike. "Whatever you guys are headed for, have fun. Maybe we'll see you again."

He revved the engine and gave them a flick of a salute while Aurora wiggled her fingers at them in goodbye. As they took off, they became a roar in the silent night. Before long, they were a shining red tail-light slowly becoming smaller and smaller down the road.

Fin only relaxed when the engine had become hardly more than an echo.

"Should we have told them about the girl?" Eryn finally let Morgan's hand go. Her skin had been clammy with sweat and she wiped it on her shorts.

Fin ran his hand over the back of his neck, gazing after them. "I mean... maybe? I just got the creeps and wanted them gone." He shuddered and folded his arms. "And they just look *familiar*. I don't know why. I was too creeped out."

At least it wasn't just Morgan then. There was something more, however. "We didn't stop for long," he whispered and Fin and Eryn faced him. "We didn't even hear them coming." He could still just barely hear the distant roar of the engine now. "We *should* have."

Maybe he shouldn't have said it, but it unnerved Morgan more than their familiarity did. No one replied. They simply turned and watched the red taillight twinkle in the dark like a distant star.

IX.
ROADSIDE MOTEL

By the time the stars had fully bloomed across the sky, they'd arrived at a small motel along the roadside. As far as Morgan could tell, it had no name beyond *Motel* which was written in neon lettering above the main office. It had exterior facing doors, a second floor with a balcony wrapped around the front, and each room had bronze number plates. Light fixtures were lit up between rooms and beyond those, the only lights were in the staircase leading up into second floor balcony, the front office, and the lone streetlight illuminating the parking lot.

Fin drove them past the office doors left open to let in the night air and parked them next to the motorcycle already there for lack of anywhere else.

Unease gnawed at Morgan's stomach as the three of them stared at the bike. It shouldn't have mattered; Vesper and Aurora were just a couple driving at night. Nothing weird. Nothing to give Morgan this horrid sense of unease like he was being followed. They couldn't have been followed; the couple had arrived at the motel earlier than they had, after all.

Eryn broke the silence with a huff. "We don't want to drive all night." She prodded Fin's shoulder with her finger. "Besides, we've slept in the car before. Not happening with three of us."

Morgan didn't have the energy to argue the point, even if he'd wanted to. The sending had left his body half-numb, tingly, and tired. It was becoming harder and harder to focus on staying awake. The road noise earlier had all but lulled him to sleep until the bright lights from the motel woke him up.

"Yeah, yeah," Fin grumbled as he pushed his door open. Eryn helped Morgan get his and they all climbed out, taking everything with them. Fin had the cooler, Eryn had two of the tote bags, and Morgan had the lightest bag. No complaint there; he might have fallen over otherwise.

The office was bright, doused in fluorescent lighting, and not very large. The front counter bisected the lobby and there was a closed room with a window behind the lone clerk. He didn't even look at them as they entered; he leaned against the counter, magazine open on his lap, and his eyes trailed to the television in the corner beside him. The sound was a hum at best and combined with the fluorescents, a headache began itching across Morgan's scalp. There was a payphone in a secluded corner near the door and flanking the other wall was a line of vending machines.

Fin went to the counter by himself, pulling out his wallet, and only then did the clerk deign to look up at them.

Eryn took Morgan to the vending machines and busied herself with looking at all the selections. Morgan wasn't really sure what to do with himself; he'd never bought anything from a vending machine before.

"Wanna try something?" She tapped the button with the orange slice on it. "This tastes like those orange and cream ice cream bars. You ever had one?"

Morgan shook his head. "I've had orange juice."

Eryn laughed and fed money into the machine. "Not the same. It's... creamier." She hit the button and it dropped into the chute at the bottom. She handed it over and debated her other options.

The can was cold and he studied it absently. Like

its button, it was an orange can with a large orange slice on the front. Not very inspiring, but his stomach needed *something* at the very least. He'd been too nervous during the drive to eat, especially after the little girl. Before he could figure out how to open it, Fin finished with the clerk and returned with a keycard.

"Upstairs," Fin said and nodded when Eryn handed him the can she'd freed for him. His had a red and blue circle on the front. "Same room we used last time, Eryn."

Her eyes lit up. "Really?" She gently nudged Morgan. "We left some withdrawn library books behind last time to give the room some reading material. Gotta see if they're still there!"

They shambled outside and headed for the stairwell. Their room wasn't far from the stairs and on the way up, Morgan was struck by how the entire place was near silent. If not for the distant road noise, there wouldn't have been anything aside from the sound of their footsteps.

Their room wasn't large by any means and smelled a bit musty. The foyer right inside had a door to the small bathroom and a little kitchen area with a sink, a small red pail, and a tiny fridge built into the counter. Past that, the room opened up enough to hold the large bed along the far wall and it faced a wooden stand that held a bulky television atop it. Beside the bed was a small couch and coffee table, splitting the room into two halves.

Eryn plopped her bags on the couch and gave the television a side-eye before she shook her head. "Don't use the TV—still costs extra here." Not that Morgan would know how to use it and he nodded. Eryn headed to the bed to check the shelves above it.

Fin left the cooler on the coffee table. "I'm gonna use the payphone downstairs," he said and shook his head as Eryn pointed at the phone on the nightstand next to the bed. "No, it's fine. I'd rather just talk to him on my own."

Morgan frowned. "Are you sure?"

Fin shrugged. "I just get grumpy when it comes to my dad and he's going to ask a million questions I don't want to answer," he said. "Stay with Eryn."

He left, closing the door behind him. Morgan listened to his footsteps quietly echo off the balcony until he was too far.

"Hey," Eryn said, bringing Morgan's attention to her. She'd turned on the lamp in the far corner of the room and it cast a comforting orange glow across everything. "Fin'll be fine. You should wash your hands and face, though. I think you'll feel better then."

Morgan gazed at his nails. He hadn't quite wiped

off all the blood; maybe she was right. He left his bag and can with the cooler and slipped into the bathroom.

Honestly, the last thing he wanted was to be left alone with his thoughts. He couldn't even deny how tired he was in the bathroom mirror, how pale he was, and just how much he still looked like the Divine, even without the veil. He cut his gaze away from himself and washed his hands, scrubbing them with the bar of soap until the blood was gone and then some more before he washed his face the same. Warm water helped.

Being alone did not. He finished up, trying to recognize himself as Morgan in the mirror—not the Divine—and after trying to wash out Fin's handkerchief to only have the blood simply smear, he came back out. Eryn was still fussing with the books, checking them over like she was looking to buy them, and hardly glanced up as Morgan went back to the couch. He sank into it and tried to empty his thoughts. He wished he knew how to bridge the silence, get Eryn talking so he didn't have to think, but he was too tired to even try.

He should have pretended he was still in solitude and did what he should have done there: focus on how absolute the Lord and Lady were. Let the worrisome thoughts go. Unfortunately, it didn't happen. The thoughts swirled, snaring him even deeper, and truth be told, he knew they'd never let go. No matter how much he believed in the Lord and Lady, it didn't matter. Not when he was so far away from the safety of the priory. Not that it had ever truly felt safe.

Maybe it was because he was finally realizing exactly what he'd done by leaving. If he never went back, his absence would doom Blackburn. Marcella couldn't do the job of two Divines. More would fall through the cracks just like the little girl.

Yet, this was the freedom he wanted. He owed everyone nothing, but even trying to acknowledge that pressed down on him as a literal weight. What did freedom *really* mean in the end? If he hadn't accepted himself as Divine, he wouldn't have helped that little girl. And yet still, here he was, trying so hard to believe he was simply Morgan—no divinity involved.

Everything felt wrong.

Eryn plopped down beside him and the motion jostled him back to reality. She'd taken a few books from the shelf and a smile played across her lips.

"Look at these!" She spread the books across the coffee table. "Most of them are still here!" She pointed at them, one by one. "There's a nice, old fantasy here, some old romances there, and ah, this one was about knighthood and chivalry."

Morgan's eyes lingered on one of the romances and his cheeks flared as he recognized the cover. A short story collection of so many different kinds of relationships. "Isn't that one a bit... um." His face grew even hotter as Eryn lifted her eyebrows. "Never mind."

Eryn jiggled his shoulder, laughing. "Since when would the clergy let you read that?"

"It was one of the ones Felicity brought me," Morgan admitted quietly.

There had been many nights Morgan stayed up late reading it when he knew no one would disturb him. If any of the clergy had caught him with it, surely there would have been words. Felicity had been eager to hear all of Morgan's opinions about everything else she'd given him, but curiously, she never asked him to elaborate on how he felt on that one in particular. Almost like she only gave it to him so he could experience something the clergy might never let him do.

The thought alone made his entire body heat up and he tried not thinking of the passages he'd memorized long before he'd buried it.

"Ah ha. We had two copies of this once and I bet that's where the other one went. I am so going to tease her when I get back." Eryn thumbed through it.

"We withdrew this one because you're not wrong... some of the stories are *very* steamy and we got a few complaints." She fanned herself and giggled when Morgan smiled at her. "Couldn't afford to offend the delicate sensibilities of old ladies looking through the shelves." She turned it and pointed at the spine. "It's definitely more worn than it was before; it's getting mileage." She set it back down, waggling her eyebrows, and Morgan had to cover his face.

"Come on," she said and stood. "We should grab some ice."

Morgan blinked. "For what?"

"Refill the cooler. It'll get too warm otherwise." Eryn collected the keycard from where Fin left it atop the cooler and headed to the door. She picked up the red pail from inside the counter's sink and beckoned Morgan over. "'Sides, it's something to do until Fin gets back. You're just going to fret otherwise." She winked when Morgan opened his mouth to dispute the fact. He closed it just as fast; maybe she was right. "Join me?"

Noise and something to do would chase away the awful feeling. Cease the buzzing in his thoughts. Smiling, Morgan took her hand.

The ice machine was back at the stairwell landing. As they walked, Morgan's gaze drifted past the balcony rail and out into the street. Something had glimmered at the edge of his vision, but nothing was actually there. His mind must have been making things up, mixing his thoughts with scant memories left behind in the motel. He held the ice bucket closer and forced himself to stay awake.

Someone was grumbling around the corner; Eryn hesitated, but it was only for a moment before she squared her shoulders and peeked around.

Aurora, the woman from the motorcycle, stood there with her bucket beneath the ice dispenser. She glared at the machine, hands on her hips while she tapped her foot. She'd changed; a comfy sheer robe was thrown over her t-shirt and now shorts. Her hair was still in its braid, but this time, Morgan sighted a vibrant red tie keeping it together.

Eryn and Morgan remained still for a moment until Aurora noticed them and then jumped with a yelp. It made Morgan jolt himself, almost dropping the pail.

"Oh!" Aurora laughed and wiggled her fingers at them in greeting. "You scared me. I'm glad you found your way here too. I almost talked Vesper into turning back to make sure you even knew it was here. Sometimes the roads aren't safe late at night." She hesitated. "I don't think I caught your names."

Her voice was so soothing and lyrical, even if all she'd said were mundane words. The world even seemed to tilt toward her, like it wanted to listen too, and Morgan had to stop himself from leaning in as well. He held tighter to the bucket, focusing on how real and tangible it was, and looked away.

"I'm Eryn and this is Morgan," Eryn said. "Fin's our other friend—he had to make a call." The words spilled out like she wasn't entirely sure if she should have introduced them, but it was too late to take it back.

Aurora nodded. "I'm Aurora and Vesper's my husband. He's gone to check for another machine."

"I'm guessing this one's broken?" Eryn drew closer to Aurora, the tension easing out of her shoulders. Morgan tried to relax too; if Eryn thought it was all right, it must have been. She poked the machine with her foot. It hummed, like nothing was wrong, but even as she pressed the button for ice, nothing came out.

Aurora pursed her lips. "I'm not sure if it's worth bothering the clerk downstairs." She leaned closer to Eryn and dropped her voice. "He's a bit surly tonight."

Eryn laughed, clapping a hand over her mouth. "Isn't he always?" She turned back to the machine and drummed her fingers on her chin.

Morgan stepped closer to look as well, but just as he did, the space between him and Aurora hummed.

The sound prickled his skin, flushing it with goose-bumps, and he grew unbelievably warm. Like someone was hugging him. The feeling was so foreign, even if the hug was as warm and loving as could be. He stepped back and it went away. No one was hugging him. Aurora didn't even seem to notice the sensation herself. The sending was messing with his mind, blending it into a dream he couldn't even see. He desperately needed sleep.

He was fully brought back to reality when Eryn's foot met the bottom of the machine with a thwack. Morgan jumped, nearly losing the bucket he'd been holding onto for dear life, and Aurora covered a gasp. The machine chugged once and then spewed out ice chunks at a rapid pace, as though making up for lost time. Eryn and Aurora erupted into laughter and Eryn dragged Morgan closer to catch the errant ice.

By the time the machine was done throwing its fit, both buckets were full. Eryn grinned, hoisting hers like she'd won a fight, and Aurora clapped, beaming.

A smile Morgan knew, deep down beyond all the fuzzy memories. Like the primordial hymn the dead sang. It made the world warm. Right. Perfectly pieced together like it was meant to be.

Until Eryn placed a hand on his shoulder and the

illusion let go, spitting Morgan back out. She steered him out of the way as he heard another set of footsteps reverberate behind them.

"Ah, you got it working?"

And the world shifted once more, becoming fuzzy and unreal, as Vesper slipped past Morgan and Eryn with just a hair's breadth between them, a certain spice smell trailing after him. Aurora raised her bucket of ice in triumph and Vesper grinned at her. He glanced down at Morgan. No. He was looking at Eryn. There was no reason he'd be looking at Morgan.

"Thank you for helping," Vesper said, his voice a soothing low tenor Morgan *knew* he'd heard somewhere before tonight. There was no doubt, but he couldn't discern *where*. "The machine down at the other end doesn't work either." He put an arm around Aurora's back. "You guys have a good night, now."

Eryn meekly waved. "You too," she said and turned to Morgan. She shoved the bucket back into his hands, the chill grounding Morgan back in reality and not some fuzzy unreality, and hurried to return to their room.

Every step away from the couple felt more and more sure, like the world was rebuilding itself beneath Morgan's feet. It only finished when the door closed behind them and they were safely inside their room. Eryn extracted the bucket from him and gave him a worried glance.

"I did not hear him coming at all," she said, a frown growing across her lips. "Aurora seems sweet, but there's something about that guy. Right down to his bleached hair. Who even *does* that?"

Morgan nodded. "Y-Yeah." His voice sounded so distant even to himself.

She hesitated, watching him still. "You okay?"

Morgan tilted his head. "Yes?" He didn't sound sure. He wasn't sure. He drew his arms across himself tightly. "Yes. I am." He had to believe it or no one would.

Eryn nodded and upturned the bucket into the cooler. The ice clinked inside, filling it, and she swore not a moment later and dunked her hands inside to extract their sandwiches. After dusting the ice off the wax paper, she left them on the top with their cans from the vending machine.

The silence was burrowing too far into Morgan's thoughts. He cleared his throat and came closer. "This place is just weird," he admitted. "They're weird."

"You're not kidding." Eryn returned the bucket to its home near the door. "Just a random motel in the middle of nowhere that's super cheap. Not complaining, though." She went to their bags and dug through them. She must have been as fidgety as Morgan. "Too far from Blackburn; too far from Rosenburg. I don't even know how it stays in business sometimes." She pulled her pajamas free and folded them neatly on the couch. "It just creepily exists in the middle somehow. We only stay here in the summer; sometimes I wonder if it exists in the other seasons."

The thought did little to soothe Morgan's worries, but he nodded all the same, trying to will away the weirdness. He reached for the tote with his borrowed sleeping clothes when someone knocked on the door. Both he and Eryn jumped and she hurried over.

"It's just me," Fin said from the other side before she could peer through the windows. She opened it up and let him in before she went back to her bag.

Morgan's entire mood brightened seeing Fin like, something felt more complete with him around, even when he appeared about as tired as Morgan felt.

"How'd it go?" Eryn asked.

The brightened mood dimmed fast, reminding Morgan of the girl in the sunflowers.

"About as well as you'd think." Fin drew a hand across the back of his neck. "My dad seemed more concerned about how the funeral went than you know, a dead little girl." When he caught Morgan's frown, he quickly shook his head. "He'll alert the right people—I promise—he just... doesn't quite have his priorities right."

"Is that all we can do?" Morgan asked as Fin came over to pass out the sandwiches.

Fin's jaw tightened. "All I got," he whispered and sat on the couch with his food. Eryn moved the tote bags to make room on the couch, but Morgan didn't want to squeeze between them. Instead, he settled himself on the edge of the bed with his food.

"Morgan," Fin said softly and Morgan hadn't realized how deeply he'd been frowning until the voice shot through him. "We didn't know a thing about her. Leaving a tip with my dad was all we *could* do."

Even if it was apparent the three of them wanted to do more. Morgan hadn't meant to sound like he blamed them for not doing enough. They had nothing to do with the girl and it wasn't like they were detectives. He simply wished he'd heard her pleas all the way in Blackburn, even if there was no way the wind could have carried it. His anger and frustration had everything to do with his own inaction about something he had no control over.

He had to get it out of his head. What he'd done

was enough. She was saved. Sent into the arms of the Lord of Night.

Yet the new silence wasn't helping. Nor did the orange and cream flavor washing down his throat once Fin opened his can for him. It fizzed and bubbled as it went, offering a new sensation Morgan wasn't sure he liked. Eryn had curled up on one end of the couch, legs underneath her, and picked at her sandwich crust. Fin had stretched his legs out, sandwich half-eaten on its wax paper in his lap. All he did was stare at the ceiling, like he was mulling over words in his head.

They wanted to say something. It weighed heavy on Morgan and he tried to focus on eating instead of the spiral their silence sent his thoughts into. Saying something wasn't inherently bad. Except it could be. He pulled pieces of the salami and cheese off and settled them in his mouth. It was taking too much energy to just eat, but he needed to. It would make his stomach feel better. Whole. Maybe it would help him feel less nervous. Maybe—

"Morgan?" Fin's voice cut through the torrent of maybes and Morgan peered up at him. "What..." He swallowed and fidgeted with the can in front of him on the table. "What happens to souls when they're left in bodies?"

Eryn nodded, mouth full from the rest of her

crust. She swallowed, still nodding. "We don't usually hear about it and even when we do, it's vague. Even fancy priory training didn't say much, right?" She nudged Fin with her foot and he waved it off.

"Just that it was paramount Divines do their job," Fin whispered.

It was an easy question, all things considered. Much better than the thousand more damning ones he'd feared. "They fester. Rot," he said, turning back to his sandwich. "They fold into the world, becoming nothing, and leave a void behind that'll just grow the more souls it eats." He picked at the bread, needing something to busy his hands with. "If you walk across a void, you feel nothing but a chill of the life already gone. You wouldn't even know what it was. There's some old battlefields rife with it still." He ceased pulling at his bread, leaving it in crumbles on the wax paper. "It's why we don't build over them..."

It was why the café that burned in Rosenburg wouldn't be built again, he realized distantly. There was the chance he hadn't sent all the dead. There was the chance they hadn't found all the bodies beneath the ash and rubble and wouldn't until it was too late. It prickled his neck, thinking of it, but it wasn't his fault. He had to stop thinking like it was.

"You just..." Morgan whispered, his voice failing him. "You just know when you step into a void where a soul has completely died. It's wrong, like you shouldn't exist either. It doesn't happen often," he added quickly, looking up at them. "Not here. Divines here are on top of things."

Except, he wasn't. The little girl was proof. Even his botched sending of Beatrice was proof. If Fin hadn't come when he did, would his house have had the void? Or would it have grown in the priory burial grounds? What kind of Divine was he if he couldn't even do this right? His eyes blurred with tears. *No*, he told himself, looking down. He was Morgan. He was more than a tool.

"Hey." Fin's voice was so close, Morgan jumped. The bed dipped with Fin's weight, but it brought Morgan back to the room. Not in his head. "It's all right."

Eryn leaned over the couch armrest. "Yeah!" she said. "Marcella's way more than enough for Rosenburg and Blackburn combined. Believe me. She's capable."

The words were meant to be comforting, Morgan was sure, but the remark hit him deep. *He* wasn't. Eryn must have realized it too; her eyes went wide, Fin shot her a long look, and Morgan ended the silence with an exhale.

"Can we not talk about it?" Morgan's voice trailed off, admitting defeat. Denial of reality. "I want to be

Morgan. Not the Divine."

"Of course," Fin said. "I'm sorry." He glanced at the clock above the door. "It's late. We'll be better tomorrow. I promise. We've got a beach and a bonfire to look forward to." He grinned and Morgan tried his hardest to match it.

"Hey, Morgan," Eryn said and he and Fin looked at her. She was looking thoughtful, a finger tapping her chin. "You've never been to a fair before, right?"

Morgan gave it some thought, but he was too tired to properly try and remember anything. He shook his head. "Not that I can remember."

Eryn faced Fin, grinning. "We should definitely take him there before we hit the beach. It might be our last chance!"

Fin sighed. "You know how crowded it gets. Though..." He smiled softly at Morgan. "If we go early enough, we should be able to dodge most of it. You want to go?" he asked. "It's just a little farther from the beach. When we were younger, my grandma always took us there first and then down to the beach when we were all tired. We can go on a few rides, play some games, eat some food, then head down for a swim and the bonfire."

Morgan nodded. "As long as you both want to go, I'll go too."

"Good!" Eryn settled back on the couch and

picked up her sandwich again. "It'll be fun! Promise!"

Though Morgan wanted to ask them more about the fair—what exactly they meant by rides, games, and food—he was too exhausted to put his thoughts back together. His body wanted him to lay down and sleep until he felt refreshed, not ask inane questions to help him ignore everything else.

They finished the rest of their sandwiches and soda quickly, and as they wrapped the trash together, Morgan caught Fin and Eryn glancing at the bed and then at the couch, like they were debating the logistics of three people in a single room.

"I can take the couch," Morgan offered and shook his head when they both were ready to argue. "I'll fit just fine. You two take the bed."

Fin still looked like he meant to convince Morgan otherwise—on the basis of what, Morgan wasn't sure because Fin surely would not fit well on the couch—but Eryn pinched his arm and he ceased. Together, they redistributed blankets and pillows from the bed. Morgan was only glad they'd remembered to pack his blanket. It was all he really needed, even though Eryn pulled an entire sheet off the bed for him.

They took turns washing up, redressing into sleep clothes, and Morgan was the first nestled in his bed on the couch. He found himself drifting off to the quiet chatter of Fin and Eryn getting ready themselves, thinking of fairs and beaches, hoping for a dreamless sleep.

X.
Nightmares at Dawn

Morgan was standing. No. That wasn't right; it couldn't be. He'd been laying on the couch, fully wrapped in blankets, wishing to dream of nothing. Yet, here he was, standing in the field of sunflowers.

Dreaming.

The sky was pitch-black, no glistening stars. The once golden sunflower petals were a ghoulish gray and as Morgan peeked between the sunflower stalks, he saw formless bodies languid and broken, ravaged by the flow of time. Skin shimmered faintly, reminiscent of a soul, but it was dull. Many of them were entrenched in place, long spindly legs buried in the dirt like roots. Many had their eyes bored from their sockets, leaving gaping black holes instead.

They were forgotten souls. Long gone out of divinity's reach.

More must have died in the field, unaware. Missing persons. Even older than Morgan. All souls he couldn't help. They cried, wailed, and the sound shook the sunflowers around them. Desperate pleas constantly lost to the world. It wasn't just sadness, however. Their anger surged wild and free, making Morgan's heart speed.

Morgan wasn't really there. He couldn't be; he'd been in the motel with Fin and Eryn and there was no way they wouldn't hear him trying to leave. Another nightmare. He drew himself tight, squeezing his eyes shut, and willed himself to wake.

The ghost of a touch grazed his bare arm and he flinched, snapping his eyes back open. Spectral fingers receded, but all the bodies had crept closer, enclosing him in a tight circle.

"W-What do you want?" Morgan whispered.

One soul lunged, latching its fingers around Morgan's wrist when he attempted to step back, and it yanked him forward. Morgan tripped, barely catching himself, and the other souls pulled at him the same. Some of them managed to hold on, their tight fingers pressing into his arms, covering the bruises the girl had made. They squeezed even tighter, like it would drag them up from the void in which they'd already fallen if they inflicted enough pain. The bruises bloomed darker, pain burrowing down into his bones, and Morgan struggled to wrench himself free.

"Let me go!" Morgan ordered, raising his voice. A soul found his throat, squeezing, and Morgan finally yanked an arm free, throwing it in front of himself. The hand released him, letting him breathe, but the sudden freedom sent him flailing backwards. He fell, the souls parting for him, and pain shot up his spine.

They loomed over him, dark eyes wide as they continued crying from mouths as dark as their eyes.

"I can't help you!" Morgan shouted, but the souls descended on him anyway. They rippled through him and into the ground, screaming, tearing bits and pieces away from him.

The world shimmered as they went, oscillating between one waterfall of memories to the next. Nothing Morgan could grasp. Spiraling darkness each time as even they had forgotten their own lives beyond their all-encompassing deaths. With each one, a spark was ignited and soon, the sunflowers around him coated themselves in fire. Each petal became a burning, golden ember in the dark of a memory that couldn't be reached.

The souls were trying to pull him under with

them, steal him away for something he could no longer give them. He forced his frozen legs to stand, taking in rapid breaths.

It wasn't even just what he couldn't give them; there was something else behind their anger. He'd taken the little girl from their clutches, what would have been a new feast, a new mind for their hive. She'd been so close and Morgan simply plucked her free, ignoring the rest. Damning them with his inaction long before he was ever Divine, ever even born. The girl was theirs and they wanted her back, especially if he couldn't save them the same.

Morgan kicked his legs free of the souls' spindly arms that had rooted him in place. They cried, breaking into pieces as his foot crashed through them, but more shot up from beneath the dirt, latching onto anything they could. Morgan stumbled again, expecting to fall outright and lose himself to the gnashing souls just below the surface, but a hand caught his. So little, but strong.

The world stopped. The flames froze, embers stilling in place in the sky like twinkling stars, and the claws digging into him slipped. The girl held his hand tight and Morgan lifted his gaze to her face. The gold from the bright flames haloed her messy black hair and she had her own sunflower tucked behind her ear. Unlike the others, it was abloom with golden petals, like the sun.

Without a word, she turned and led him away from the crying souls. Her presence alone gave him the strength he lacked, and step by step, she drew him away. The souls stayed rooted in the dirt, their cry slowly growing into silent whimpers, and the girl kept walking. She took him through the smoldering sunflowers until the world came back.

Stars unveiled themselves first, each one bright, and soon new sunflowers sprouted from the ash and soot. Petals unfurled, bright and golden, and turned toward an unseen sun.

She faced Morgan only then and took the sunflower from her hair. She reached up and Morgan had to bend down for her to slide the bud into his. When she finished, she was still smiling.

"Thank you," she mouthed, no voice coming forth.

And a spectral hand took hers and her eyes fluttered shut. Yet her smile remained even as the Lord of Night lifted her into his arms. Asleep to dream of the dawn the Lady would grant her. She was saved, nestled against the Lord's shoulder as he wrapped his shawl of stars around her like a blanket.

The Lord of Night looked at Morgan so clearly, it had to be more than a nightmare. It was too stark, too real; he *knew* Morgan had left the priory. His star-filled gaze pierced through Morgan and a question resounded in the air: *why?*

Morgan wanted to shout it right back.

The warm hand on his shoulder stopped him; the world receded, becoming a blur of moving shapes, and Morgan jolted awake. The motel ceiling greeted him, but so did the warm hand now pressed against his cheek.

Morgan stilled, holding his breath, and glanced to his side. Fin was bending over him, sleepy in the early morning light. He pressed the back of his hand to Morgan's forehead next before he noticed Morgan staring.

"Sorry." Fin jerked his hand away like he'd been burned. "You looked feverish and didn't wake up when I shook you." He sat on the floor beside the couch, rubbing his eyes. "You okay?"

Morgan settled softly into the pillow. His heart was calming in his chest, but it felt like he'd been running all night. Morgan met Fin's worried gaze with a faint smile. "Just a bad dream," he whispered. "Nothing more."

Fin watched him, warm brown eyes bright against the dim light from the window. Morgan had to look away, his face hot, and Fin rested his head against Morgan's arm.

"You still *look* feverish."

Morgan released his arm and pushed Fin's head away, laughing. "Stop it," he said and all Fin did was keep on grinning teasingly. A grin Morgan had known. Somewhere, deep down in a hole of memory. Too far gone to grasp. "W-What time is it?"

"Too early," Fin groaned, stretching his arms over his head. And Morgan realized Fin was not wearing a shirt and though he'd gone to simply *look* at Fin, just to make sure he wasn't imagining it, Morgan quickly redirected his stare at the ceiling instead. His body was on fire. Maybe he *was* feverish.

"Clock says seven," Fin said. "Bet Eryn won't be up for a bit. She likes sleeping in."

If Morgan was back at the priory, he'd be just rising for another day of solitude. If he would have survived without Fin. The thought left him cold, washing the heat from his body, and he tried to brush it away. The what ifs didn't matter. What did was that he was alive and was with Fin.

"Was it about the girl?" Fin asked and Morgan peered at him again. "Do you think writing it down will help?"

Morgan tilted his head. "You mean her memories?" He thought a moment and nodded. It couldn't hurt. "Maybe. Do you have some paper and something to write with?"

There was a smile on Fin's own lips as he

reached for the totes beside the couch. There was a little digging, a black and white tank top pulled out first, and then a small, very well-loved notebook with a pen wedged inside. Though Morgan craned his neck to see what else the notebook had in it, Fin flipped past it too fast and handed the whole thing over.

"It's just photo composition ideas. Grandma said sketching them sometimes might help me take a better shot," Fin said before Morgan could chance a peek. "Feel free to take as many pages as you need, though. Haven't really been sketching lately."

Yet he brought the notebook all the same. Morgan resolved to not take many at all—memories seldom needed more than a page or two at most— and sat up with his back against the armrest. As he situated himself, Fin had stood and faced away to pull on his tank top. Morgan took a selfish moment to trace the muscles in Fin's back with his eyes before they were covered. Immediately, Morgan's face flushed and he hastened to concentrate on the blank page in his lap instead.

No name came to mind. Barely even her face even though Morgan could still see her smile. The rest was shrouded in shadows and what might have been. Maybe freckles, black hair, but hardly any more. The rest of the details ran away each time

Morgan searched for them. Even with the pen poised, begging the memory to recall itself so he could write *something*, it remained stubbornly distant. He sighed and fell against the couch pillow.

"Not working?" Fin asked. He'd sat back down beside the couch, watching Morgan.

"It's not coming," Morgan whispered. "I *could* just write what I remember, but that's not how the process works. If her memories won't guide my hand, it won't take ownership and it'll stick with me."

Fin tilted his head and rested his cheek on his palm, thinking. "Is it because she was already almost gone?"

"Maybe." Morgan handed the notebook and pen back. "I'll be fine." He fidgeted as Fin continued to watch him, worried. "W-What are you doing up?"

"I had to pee," Fin said as he slid the notebook back into its tote. "Figured I could get us breakfast since I was up."

"I see."

Fin rested an arm back on the couch. "Do you want to talk about the bad dream? Would that help?"

No. He didn't. Morgan released another sigh, hoping it was answer enough, but Fin didn't stop watching him. Maybe talking *would* help, even if it never had before. Fin was different than the clergy, at least. He wouldn't just suggest milk tea to make it go away.

"People die all the time," Morgan said. "It's mortality. We will die as much as we've lived." He quoted a line of scripture itching in his head. Something grounding even though he was so far away from Divine doctrine now. "Sometimes, lives fester and rot, and we can't do anything about it." He looked down at his arms where the bruises had darkened. Fingers crisscrossing over one another in a hideous shade of purple and blue stark against his pale skin. He hid them underneath the blanket before Fin noticed. "There were other souls where she died—I don't know how many. Maybe one very angry one? A few? However many it was, they were angry I sent the little girl and reached into my dreams to let me know."

"Other souls?"

"People die all the time," Morgan repeated softly. "Whether we acknowledge it or not. She wasn't the only one forgotten." Perhaps she wouldn't be the last, but he hesitated saying it aloud. "And they want their void to grow. They don't want to be left alone in their suffering. All they want is more."

Maybe it wasn't the right thing to say. Fin had gone silent and Morgan let it settle between them until it made him nervous.

"I'm sorry," Morgan said and Fin lifted his

eyebrows. "Writing would have kept them at bay if I'd known more about her. I think they reached out because she's still lingering in my head. I don't mean to scare you." No one liked thinking about death and mortality.

Fin shook his head. "Nah," he said. "That's not scary. Now, if you killed one of us, yeah, then that'd scare me away." It was such a ridiculous concept, Morgan laughed, quickly lifting his hands to smother the sound. Fin smirked at him and Morgan's face grew even hotter.

The good cheer didn't last long; Fin's gaze dropped to the bruises and he frowned. Morgan didn't have time to hide them; Fin gently took one of his hands and held it steady so he could look.

"Sometimes manifestations become realer than they are," Morgan whispered. "It's fine. I can deal with it."

It was the first time he'd *had* to, but if bruises were all he got, then he figured he could deal with it. Fin didn't look quite convinced and Morgan cut his gaze away, trying to hide his arm beneath the sleeve. Out of sight; out of mind.

"Do you want some air?" Fin asked.

Morgan lifted his eyebrows. "Hm?"

Fin shrugged. "To clear your head. It's still bothering you, isn't it?" As Morgan mulled over the words, Fin shook his head. "I mean all of this. Send-ings and everything."

Maybe air *would* help and he nodded, although he wondered at the same time if it was just a way to talk more without waking up Eryn. Even now, she rolled over as though just realizing the bed was all hers and promptly took it over with a soft, satisfied sigh.

Morgan gently extracted himself from his blankets, settled his cap loosely on his head, and let Fin lead him out the door. The chill of the morning air ghosted across his cheeks and bare legs as he stepped onto the balcony, but it was refreshing. Washed away any lingering heat from imaginary fires.

Fog snaked across the parking lot and street, some of it catching scant sunlight from behind them, but other than that, the motel looked much the same as it had last night.

Fin left the door open a crack and leaned on the balcony railing, clasping his hands together. More and more, he looked like he wanted to say some-thing. Morgan let him think and rested beside him, casting his gaze across the balcony. He stopped at the room on the far end of the other side and he bit the inside of his cheek. Vesper was leaning against the balcony as well, cigarette balanced in his fingers. The smoke trailed upward like a fog of its own. Vesper noticed them after a moment and gave them a little wave before he turned away, like he was giving them privacy. Morgan gave him the same and turned so he was facing Fin.

Except Fin still hadn't begun speaking. Morgan drummed his fingers softly against the paint chipping off the railing and swallowed. Someone had to start. "You look like you want to say something," he said.

"Why is it all on you?" Fin whispered, but he wouldn't look up from his hands. "Why on the hundreds of other Divines? Why not on the Lord and Lady themselves?"

Morgan shook his head. "Scripture states the Lord and Lady vowed not to interfere. They were but guiding hands, watching the world they made from stardust grow and prosper."

Fin raked his hair back with both hands and exhaled sharply. Morgan frowned. It mirrored his own frustration with the very same scripture.

"That's bullshit. Just having Divines at all interferes," Fin argued. "If we die and rot, well, that's the nature of the world they made. They're already interfering by forcing people like you to ferry us. They're already involved."

A headache prickled at the corner of Morgan's

vision and he drew himself tighter. "If nothing helped the dead cross, imagine how dark the world would be."

"But why does it need to come at the expense of you?" Fin faced Morgan, his expression taut with worry. "Morgan—look at your arms. How many memories have you had to lose because they expect *you* to deal with the dead?" The words played in Morgan's head with a similar argument made once upon a time. "How much do they expect you to do before you fall apart because of some god who won't do his own job? Does he even care? Is he actually even *there?*"

There was anger behind Fin's words, ones Morgan felt just as warmly, but it left him frustrated rather than anything useful. Fin was watching him for a reply—he must have been the way his eyes hadn't left Morgan's—and when Morgan hesitated giving one, Fin opened his mouth again.

"Please, stop." Morgan's voice came out sharper than he meant, but Fin stammered into silence all the same. "What exactly do you want me to say?" he asked, words trembling as they followed a memory he couldn't quite parse. "I don't have the privilege to think like you do. Divines have to do what they do so the whole cycle continues and I can't stand here and pretend it's not a *real* thing." He felt his throat with shaking fingers. "Every time I do a sending, do you know what happens to me? Physically?" A door shut somewhere across the balcony, softly like it meant not to interrupt them, and Fin didn't look away from Morgan. "The Lord of Night reaches into my throat for the soul. I can *feel* it. You can say he's not real, but I know he is."

"Morgan—"

"I've already turned my back on the priory by leaving," Morgan continued, Fin's voice but a distant echo in the back of his head. His entire body trembled as he forced himself to hold Fin's gaze. "I don't know *why* the Lord of Night does not—cannot do this by himself. I don't know why he trusts me to do this when I barely can." He squeezed his eyes shut, willing away the headache flooding over his vision, and turned to rest his back against the railing, finally looking away. "I barely even helped that girl. Even your grandmother. I can't even do the simplest task like writing down the damn memories right. But it has to be done. It just has to be."

He hadn't meant to let all the words spill out. All it did was highlight his own indecision. He was escaping, but on the same coin he couldn't. Not really. Morgan pressed his palms against his eyes, willing the tears back, and the headache only worsened until a warm hand touched his wrist.

Morgan let it take his hand away to simply hold.

"Morgan," Fin repeated softly. It made butterflies stir inside Morgan's stomach, but they fled with how sad Fin was watching him. "I'm sorry. I didn't mean to say all that. I just... I get frustrated. And I shouldn't have taken it out on you." He glanced away and shook his head. "In my house, when you gave me the scalpel, I realized they weren't helping you at all." He squeezed Morgan's hand. "It's not fair they thrust this and their entire moralistic guilt on you and then lock you in solitude all by yourself, regardless if it *has* to be done." He finally looked at Morgan again, brown eyes clear. "You are not their plaything to do something they refuse to do themselves." He leaned in closer, his voice quieter with each word, like he'd face divine punishment otherwise. "You are allowed to be selfish—it's *your* life."

Despite the blasphemy of the speech, Morgan found his anger melting away and allowed himself a smile. "Is this why I've never seen you at Holy Day Mass or at any holiday?" he said, tilting his head closer. "Would you have been compelled to save me from being Divine?"

Fin laughed, leaning back, and Morgan stopped himself from huffing. He wasn't sure what he'd been expecting, but it wasn't that. Acknowledging he'd expected anything else at all, however, made his face warm.

"Hey," Fin said and let his hand go. "I'm not welcome back, remember? One and only guy who got fired." He grinned teasingly and Morgan rolled his eyes. "My grandma got on me about that too, you know? Except I'd always bake her cookies while she was gone. How could she stay mad after that? Want me to bake you something to cheer you up? I make a mean oatmeal cookie."

Laughter trickled out of Morgan's throat, the remnants of the argument fizzling altogether, and Fin leaned in again. This time it was so quick, Morgan was too slow to react, and Fin pressed his lips to Morgan's cheek, kissing it. He withdrew just as fast, eyes wide like he'd done something wrong, and Morgan was sure Fin's shock mirrored his own.

"I'm going—" Fin cleared his throat and suddenly patted down his jeans. He found the keys in one pocket and yanked them out. "I'm gonna get us some breakfast from that gas station just down the bend." He nodded toward their door as he made a wide arc around Morgan to get to the stairs. "See if you can get Eryn up for me, okay?" Another smile in Morgan's direction and he turned away. "I'll be back soon."

And just like that, Fin hurried to the stairwell and descended. Morgan wasn't sure if his haste was out of sheer embarrassment or something else. Nevertheless, Morgan smiled, pressing a hand to his cheek, and watched as Fin backed out of the parking space and headed out of the lot.

Had someone else kissed him on the same cheek before? Fin had left him feeling unbelievably warm and loved, but it wasn't a foreign emotion. It really felt like someone had done the same before.

As Morgan ruminated on the phantom memory trying to surface, he headed into their room, and only realized he must have had a silly look on his face when he sighted Eryn just inside, hands on her hips with a teasing grin.

"Ah," Eryn said and Morgan's entire face went hot. "I know that look. He must have kissed you on the cheek." She returned to the bed and pulled the sheets in a half-attempt to make it neater. "Fin's been giving you that look all the time when you aren't looking, you know."

"No." Morgan laughed, face even hotter. "He hasn't been!"

"Uh huh. He totally has."

Morgan hurried across the room and Eryn held up her hands in surrender. "No way—I think I'd know."

Except, immediately after denying it so vehemently, he thought of the first photo he'd taken with Fin. The way Fin had unknowingly caught himself staring at Morgan with an expression that *still* made Morgan's entire body buzz.

Eryn snorted and rolled her eyes. "That's what I thought. Have you ever kissed anyone before?" Somehow, Morgan's face felt hotter. Maybe he was on fire. "It's a little different than reading about it, you know. Want me to warn him?" She giggled as Morgan pressed his face into his hands and turned away to sink into the couch.

"Oh, come on!" She raced after him. "Why are you *that* red? Have you? That'd be the scandal of Blackburn!"

Morgan mumbled a weak "shut up" and rested the back of his head against the cushion. Something in the fuzzy depth of memory had lit up when she'd asked him. Eryn gently sat next to him, expectant. What could he say? Maybe, but with the warning it might not even be his memory? Just one he selfishly kept because it was the only way he'd ever know how it felt? Except... Morgan felt his lips. The vague memory persisted, becoming a tangible whisper resounding in his thoughts.

The cloth of his veil pushed against his lips as someone leaned in, draped in black.

It was *there*. Stark details only he'd have as Divine. He put his hand down suddenly, eyes wide, and found Eryn's eyebrows were high on her forehead.

"Are you serious?" she whispered.

"H-Have *you*?" Morgan asked, deflecting to gather his words.

Eryn snorted and slapped her knee. "I have, actually! Quite a few times!" She thankfully took her expectant gaze away and stretched out her legs in front of her. "My first time was with Fin when we were thirteen. People always said we'd be cute together, but well... there were absolutely no sparks. Honestly? A let down." She quickly waved her hand in front of her. "Not to say he's a bad kisser now! Not with how often he and his ex insisted on kissing." She dropped her hands in her lap with a plop, abruptly stopping the train of thought.

"When I went to the city earlier this year for my university's orientation, I met this other girl in my program." Her voice had turned soft with a smile to match." We might have kissed. A few times. *Many* times. It was the first time I'd found another girl who also liked girls." Her cheeks tinged with pink and she covered her face for a moment before she turned to jostle Morgan's knee.

"Come on, spill. Your face is *so* red. Was someone really ballsy enough?"

Definitely on fire, Morgan was sure of it. He

swallowed and shrugged one shoulder. "I-It's fuzzy, but it has to be mine because I can remember my veil and his lips against it." He felt his face again, suddenly aware of its absence. "He was wearing black—he must have been my attendant after Felicity?" The more he spoke, the more the memory attempted to solidify. Unfortunately, it stubbornly remained as a mere brush of details.

The vividness of the way the young man's lips pressed against Morgan's was the lone constant. The way his veil had prevented them from truly touching. Singing through the simple image was even the way Morgan had *enjoyed* it. Another memory tried to bubble up, chasing after the first, and Morgan's heart raced.

"He just planted one on you?" Eryn asked, bridging Morgan back to reality. Her eyes were wide and she was covering her mouth. "No lead up?"

"He must have been flirting with me before-hand," Morgan said and more details snapped into focus. Shy smiles turning into bold, teasing grins. The way he'd tapped Morgan's foot underneath the table until Morgan tapped it back. The smallest, softest touches when no one was looking. "I was stunned when it happened, because I didn't under-stand why my heart fluttered whenever I got to see him until then." He smiled even as his stomach filled with the butterflies he must have felt then too.

The other memory finally surfaced as a bold declaration there had been another time. Morgan hated he couldn't make out concrete details. "Then," he began haltingly and tried to ignore how Eryn practically vibrated beside him with excitement, "I think he kissed me a second time."

Eryn whistled. "I can't believe the Lord of Night didn't smite him!"

Morgan laughed quietly. There was the evening sun setting behind the priory. The light had shimmered across what Morgan could see of the young man's skin, coating it in a golden bronze. The tree in the burial ground had shadowed them beneath the leaves rustling in the warm summer breeze. It could have been *any* memory, Morgan tried to reason it away, but the next detail cemented it. He'd shown the young man his teeth ("Are they really that sharp? Can I see them?" asked so coyly and softly). And then...

"He wanted to see my teeth," Morgan said, distantly. "I moved my veil aside and showed him. I guess I wasn't scared of doing something so blasphemous then. And then he kissed me underneath it."

Was there more? He begged his memories to give him more—there had to be—but it was just those two. Nothing else unburied itself. It was certainly enough for Eryn, at least. She'd gone from total excitement to watching him contently, leaning her cheek on her palm.

"Aw," she cooed. "That's actually really suave and sweet. What happened to him?"

He disappeared. The gaping hole in Morgan's memory refused to give him up. A hole where he should have been. "I don't know. He left, I guess."

The ending didn't sound right in Morgan's head. There was something incomplete beyond someone leaving because they wanted to do something else. A sensation begged Morgan to think harder of the memories he'd forgotten, but no matter how hard he tried, there was nothing else.

Eryn must have felt the same let down; she frowned, drumming her fingers on her chin in thought. After a moment of fidgeting, she sidled closer to Morgan and lowered her voice. "Okay, hear me out for a second. That wouldn't have been Fin, right?"

Morgan straightened, eyes wide.

"I mean," Eryn added quickly, holding her hands in front of her, "he never told me *why* the priory kicked him out or hell, *what* he'd even been doing for the priory. But I remember how crushingly sad he was after the fact. Our last year of school, he was back and forth in the priory's training and then after he graduated, for almost an entire year, he worked there saying how much he liked it despite... you know, not being very religious."

How long was the memory gap? Morgan tried to place it, but he couldn't. Nebulously between now and when Felicity left. Days were always a blur, a haze, and he couldn't say for sure. What bothered him more than not being able to remember, however, was Fin's silence.

"Why wouldn't he say anything?" Morgan asked.

"Maybe because *you* didn't remember *him*," Eryn suggested. "He told me he dropped through the roof on you. If he started with saying he knew you? Wouldn't you have panicked?" She waited and Morgan slowly nodded. "He flirts a *lot*, but he doesn't flirt with you nearly as much as he has with others. Maybe he figured if *you* didn't remember, he didn't want to push it until you did."

Assuming it was Fin at all. Typically, Divine attendants wore cowls covering their faces from the nose up. Their lips were in plain view, the idea that they were meant to be the Divine's mouthpiece. He'd seen Felicity's glasses many times because she'd constantly cleaned them on her issued robes and her hair had a way of escaping the cowl.

But the second attendant? The maybe Fin? All Morgan recalled vividly was the lips. And Fin's continued to be familiar for reasons Morgan still couldn't parse. Even still, Morgan must have known his name like he'd known Felicity's. Why hadn't the memories come tumbling back when Fin introduced himself?

Eryn gently pressed a hand to Morgan's arm.

"I'm going to repeat my caveat: I might be wrong," she said. "Maybe I shouldn't have mentioned it, but I just felt that there's something there. The way he watches you when you aren't paying attention? It's like he really does know you." She withdrew her hand. "But I might be wrong. Maybe I'm making this up because I think you'd be cute together."

Morgan snorted and nodded. "Thank you," he said. "I just—" He couldn't stop the sigh leaving his throat. "My memories are so jumbled. I'm never really sure what's *mine*. Those two? They feel so much like mine; I want them to be so badly."

"For what it's worth..." Eryn reached up and took Morgan's hat off his head to tuck a lock of hair behind his ear. It was something so sisterly, it caught him completely off guard. A trickle of memory flickered to life, but it had no substance. Just a feeling. "I agree with Fin. Nothing's wrong with you being selfish. The souls of the dead should never rest on one person alone, no matter how small that city is. You should be allowed to live just as much as us. As anyone."

"Oh, you were listening?"

Eryn chuckled. "You left the door open a crack and I'm nosy. I'm serious, though." She stressed the words and watched Morgan. "When I think back to when Fin and I were twelve? All we did was ride bikes and catch frogs. At twelve you'd already given up your childhood so you could send the dead into the afterlife." She frowned and Morgan had to look away, suddenly feeling tears begin to well up. "You know, it never really dawned on me how young you were until I saw you at the spring service a few years ago."

Marking the first day of spring, the Vernal Equinox Service was typically held outside in the priory gardens. The first flowers of spring would be in bloom and it was customary for citizens of Blackburn to bring flowers of their own to join the priory's garden. Morgan didn't remember any particular service very well, but he'd always enjoyed the fresh air after being cooped up inside all winter.

"Me and Fin had brought some of his grandmother's flowers to share on her behalf," Eryn continued slowly, her gaze distant as she thought back. "Felicity must have been your attendant then—I remember a woman beside you with black hair escaping her hood. She was like a bubbly barrier between you and everyone else. You stayed beside her, not looking at anyone until this little girl got past her and gave you a chrysanthemum she'd kept alive all winter."

Try as Morgan might, he couldn't recall any little girl giving him a flower of any kind. It hurt him deeper than he thought it would to have someone who had shown him an ounce of friendliness only for him to forget about it. Misplacing the memory entirely.

"I don't remember," Morgan whispered, his voice trembling.

"You looked confused taking the flower." Eryn considered Morgan sadly. "But Felicity tucked it into your hood and the girl was so happy, she hugged you. You didn't respond much, but the girl didn't mind." She unclasped her hand and reached one over to squeeze Morgan's arm. "Fin asked one of the clergypersons nearby why you looked so sad then and they just said it was how you were. Distant. Neither of us really believed that—you were just young and lonely, so desperately in need of a friend. I think Felicity tried her best." She gave him a faint smile. "Maybe a month later, the prior came to the school offering graduates a job. Fin must have put two-and-two together, figuring it was to be your attendant, and applied regardless if he was religious.

He wanted to be your friend."

A slow breath eased out of Morgan, shaking like he was, and he tried so hard to blink back tears. Eryn rubbed his arm.

"Whatever happens, we're your friends, Morgan," she said. "And if you want to be selfish, we'll be right here to help you do just that."

The sentiment made him cry. Maybe it was bound to happen. Maybe he'd been on the edge of it for such a long time. It was different than at Fin's house. This was complete relief—letting go—where there, it had been desolation. Eryn slid her arm across his back and pressed him close and Morgan only found more tears washing down his cheeks despite his effort to stop them and insist he was fine.

He'd known them for so little, but everything they'd done and said meant more than whatever doctrine and scripture he'd had to read to find solace. Their simple friendship already felt like a lifetime.

XI.
Fog in the Morning

⌐⟋⟍¬

Eryn convinced Morgan to take the bathroom first to clean up and he appreciated it after all the crying. Though his eyes were still a little red after he'd washed up and changed, he'd managed to clear his nose and felt some modicum of normal. He was real in the mirror this time—himself.

All he needed to do was figure out how to talk to Fin—*really* talk to him and draw out the truth. Everything made sense in Eryn's context, somehow suddenly stark because he'd fully acknowledged it, refusing to let the memories sink below the others this time, and he wanted it so badly to be true. It'd be an answer to the fuzzy images igniting to life whenever he was near Fin.

At the same time, however, what if Eryn was

wrong? Morgan feared bringing it up at all if it ruined what friendship he and Fin had now.

When he left the bathroom, Eryn had already packed most of their things except a change of clothes for herself. She smiled seeing him and held out her arms to take his sleeping clothes.

"Better?" she asked as she slipped them into Fin's bag.

Morgan returned her smile. "Much. Thank you."

As Eryn went to pass him with her own clothes, a knock resounded from the door. It was gentle and soft, like it feared waking them, and they stilled. If it was Fin returning, he would have said something already. The door was locked, thank goodness, but it did little to put Morgan at ease when the knock came once more in their silence, simply louder.

"Ah... Mr. Thorne?" a tired voice from outside called. Eryn threw her clothes down and pushed Morgan toward the window in the back. "This is management. I know it's early, but you awake in there?"

"He's out!" Eryn winced as soon as she'd spoken. She shot a wild look at Morgan, eyes wide, and he shook his head. It wasn't like either of them could have mimicked Fin's voice; it was too low. "W-We were just getting ready to leave. I thought checkout was at noon."

"Well, that's not it," the voice continued. "Someone's here to talk to him. And you, I guess, since you're with him." The balcony creaked as someone stepped back. "They're from Blackburn. Said they drove all night to catch you."

The world was suddenly so small and miniscule. Morgan's pulse raced, pounding in his ears. They couldn't have followed him. No. It wasn't possible they *knew*.

Except, he hadn't been careful. Anyone could have seen him waiting for Felicity. Sitting in the car. On the ride down. And there was a *hole* in the spire's roof. It was a miracle they'd gotten this far at all.

Another voice spoke on the other side of the door. "Someone very dear is missing."

Morgan wanted to throw up, but instead his body went even stiffer, and he couldn't breathe. The Head Prior. He was here.

Morgan forced a breath in, a wheeze at most, and Eryn shot him another panicked look. Morgan shook his head. She couldn't open the door. He'd be caught. He had nowhere to hide; they'd search the whole room.

"I am Prior Augustus from Blackburn," he continued, answering Eryn's silence as though it was a question of his validity. "Can we speak with you? We only mean to find this individual. It won't take long."

"You can speak to me through the door," Eryn shot back as she went for the window beside Morgan. It took both of them to get it open and when they did, the smell of the pine trees around the motel rushed inside.

"Everyone else here has been so cooperative," Augustus said slowly as Eryn peered downward. "Please. Just open the door and I'll be quickly out of your hair. I can wait until Mr. Thorne comes back, if you prefer." He waited a beat. "I also have Sister Lindsey with me if it makes you feel safer. I mean you no harm."

The name didn't ring a bell. It brought to mind no faces, just another clergy member right under Augustus' thumb. Morgan peered out the window. The pine trees were pressed up close. He *could* climb. It wasn't like scaling down the spire's walls, rather going from branch to branch. Couldn't have been hard, especially since when compared to the spire, they weren't *that* high. He swallowed and indicated his plan to Eryn and though she gritted her teeth like it was the last plan she wanted him to do, she nodded.

"Just—Just let me get a freakin' bra on," Eryn called out and went back to her pile of clothes. She tossed them across the room haphazardly. "I'd hate to stop your search, but I really *should* be decent."

"Why, of course. Take your time," Augustus said.

He fully expected to find Morgan hiding some-how—trapped inside with no way out—no matter how long Eryn stalled, except he wouldn't. There *was* a way out. Morgan gingerly slipped his legs out the window, sitting on the ledge, and afforded himself a deep breath before he went for the first branch. He had to push through the nettles, but the branch easily held his weight as he secured his legs around it.

Eryn came over. "Don't go far," she whispered, hardly audible, and closed the window.

Cutting him off. It scared him more than he thought it would, being completely on his own. It *was* his idea, though, and he couldn't take it back now. He heard Eryn's muffled annoyance beyond the window—"where is that blasted bra? I just had it!"—before he gently lowered himself to the next sturdy branch below.

At each one, he took a break for a deep breath, holding tight to the branch for dear life. He probably didn't have to go all the way to the ground, but he didn't want to chance waiting and being found by someone peeking out another window. He kept going, branch by branch until he could drop safely. When his feet hit the ground, he fell against the tree to catch his breath. His arms were shaking, legs wobbling, and the breeze through the trees made him cold.

But he was free. That was what mattered.

If Augustus was convinced he was there, however, surely they'd check around the motel when they didn't find him in the room. Glancing up at the window, he saw no sign of Eryn and breathed out. He wouldn't go far, just enough into the trees where no one would think he'd go.

It was silent so early in the morning and still a little dim, but dawn light filtered through the gaps between the pines and oaks, settling around the area in a kind of ethereal gold that made him feel right at home. The fog was thicker back here as it circled the tree trunks, but it wasn't oppressive or frightening. It was almost like he wasn't on the run from the clergy, rather simply on a walk by himself through the priory cemetery.

At least, until he heard voices through the trees. They dragged him right back to reality and he hurried further in, careful to keep his steps light. The footsteps followed him and his panic wound back up, making his chest tight. He didn't know which direction they were coming from.

Twigs crunched underfoot behind Morgan. Branches were brushed aside, nettles crinkling as they moved while the footsteps became faster. The earlier peace ripped away, replacing itself with ter-ror. Everything was the same in all directions. The hush of trees, the echo of footsteps, and his own panicked breathing. Morgan rounded a large oak and hid behind it, growing as still as he could between the roots jutting out of the ground. Maybe if *he* stopped making noise, however slight, his pursuer would move on, thinking he'd just been an animal scurrying away in the morning.

He settled his back against the bark and as soon as it touched, memories washed over him, flushing goosebumps all the way down. He'd been running and hiding before in the woods, but it wasn't out of terror. He'd stifled his laughter as a man wondered aloud where he could have gone. The man had found him only because Morgan couldn't keep quiet. His face wouldn't come, just the warmth of his smile when he came around the tree, and how Morgan had squealed with delight as the man held him high on his shoulder.

Tears dampened Morgan's cheeks as he blinked, bringing the reality of the pines in the fog back into focus. A man with glasses was kneeling in front of him now. Morgan bit back a shout, feeling the sting of his teeth, and threw one arm out, the other one pushing off the tree. The man caught his arm, holding it steady, and held up his other hand.

"Hey—hey," he said softly. "It's just me."

Morgan looked at him, really looked at him even

though panic screamed at him to shove and run. The warm eyes caught his attention first. The way the black-rimmed glasses practically glimmered in the light. Then his black hair peppered with white and gray. He wore the typical clergy cassock, almost a literal shadow in the foggy haze. It took Morgan another moment before he gasped, full recognition snapping into place. The escort who had been with him in the morgue. The one who'd tried to stand up for him to the Head Prior that same night.

Though his name wouldn't come, the warmth of his voice echoed in Morgan's head. Perhaps he could be reasoned with.

Morgan took a deep breath and shook his head. "Don't tell—"

"I won't," the man said, gently letting Morgan go. He waited a moment, like he expected Morgan to say something else, but when he didn't, he propped an elbow on his knee and rested his chin on his palm. "Your Holiness—"

"My name is Morgan," he said through gritted teeth. None of that. Never again.

He fully expected annoyance. A sigh. A refusal to use a name that was *his*. Reducing him right back to the tool they were looking for, but the man only nodded.

"Morgan." He spoke it so softly, Morgan relaxed.

The man held out his hand. "My name is Joseph. I don't mind that you don't remember it—I understand."

Yet Morgan did. Vaguely. Except he'd simply forgotten who the name had belonged to and gave it to a long-gone memory. He slowly took Joseph's hand and Joseph gave it a firm shake. He was happy to let go and wrapped both arms around his knees, curling up to keep hiding.

"Harmony is the redhead usually tailing me," Joseph said, answering a question Morgan had only begun to form in his head. "She doesn't mind it either. She's on lookout. You're pretty fast, you know that? And I understand."

"No. You don't," Morgan said and Joseph frowned. "You can leave whenever you want to. I am not going back. Not now. Not with you."

His friendliness was a ruse. Waiting for Morgan to drop all guard to strike. Morgan knew he wasn't heavy. If Joseph really wanted to, he could have just grabbed Morgan and carried him back to wherever the priory cab was. It wasn't like there was anyone around witness them stuffing the Divine in the back of a cab.

But the hurt was too real on Joseph's expression. He watched Morgan in silence, searching his face, until he finally sat down in front of him, rubbing his knees. "I know," he said again. He was older than Morgan thought; the golden dawn rays lit how exhausted he was, the few fine lines etched around his eyes. "I can only speak for myself of course, but I *was* incredibly worried seeing the state of your room. Although now, I see you are well cared for."

Morgan tightened his arms around his knees, still watching Joseph suspiciously. "No one's worried about *me*. Just about the Divine."

"You are one in the same," Joseph stressed sadly. "I can't change that. No one can."

If he didn't go back, Morgan could change it. The lie didn't sit well with Morgan, however; even he knew no matter how far he ran, he'd still be Divine. Instead of answering, he glanced away.

"Someone from Blackburn saw the hole yester-day afternoon." Joseph folded his hands in his lap. "She was elderly and incredibly worried you'd been hurt. We assured her you were not, and when we didn't find you in the rubble after with the window open, Augustus put two and two together. We haven't told anyone else you're missing, though. He didn't want to cause a panic." He tilted his head to one side, like he was trying to get Morgan to look at him again. "Augustus was..." He eased out a sigh. "You know how he is—a man possessed. He made us drive all night."

Not because he was worried, but because he was mad. Morgan had the audacity to escape. A dark thought wondered how Augustus would have felt finding something else instead and Morgan instantly dashed it back.

"How'd you know I'd be here?"

Joseph adjusted his glasses. "Augustus has a chip on his shoulder concerning Mr. Thorne. For some reason, he just *knew* he'd somehow helped you. When we didn't find anyone at Mrs. Thorne's house, Augustus asked around. All the neighbors said around this time each year, she'd take her grandson out this way and surmised Mr. Thorne was taking one more trip in light of her funeral. Honestly, I didn't think Augustus would be right even when the neighbors said they saw a new face with Fin."

"It's my fault," Morgan whispered. "It was me. Please. I asked him to help."

"I am not punishing anyone," Joseph said, lowering his voice. "Harmony and I agreed that if we found you out here, we'd let you choose."

"Why?"

"Because in the end, it's your life." Joseph leaned back, looking away finally, and set his gaze on the pines where the golden light had made a halo around them. "I don't understand the power or why it had to come to this. Lilia often escaped on her own during solitude; she was masterful at climbing those walls. We allowed her these excursions because it made her happy." His face had grown increasingly soft at the edges. He must have been her attendant; he would have been the right age. "When it was time, I always showed her home." He swallowed and shook his head. "And yet, Augustus keeps you locked inside, firing any attendant you genuinely grow to like. His word is too absolute and anything we've done to help falls on deaf ears."

Morgan stayed silent and studied Joseph. He'd never really taken note of the man before. All he'd been was another clergyperson trying to control Morgan under the guise of help. Unlike all the others who stopped trying as soon as Morgan showed any resistance, Joseph had kept trying, eventually leading Harmony to do the same. Little gestures here and there. Dressing his bed when it wasn't their job. Volunteering to go with him before Augustus assigned someone Morgan didn't even know. Even the milk tea was from a place of genuine kindness. And Morgan had never bothered to memorize their names.

"You," he whispered, a sudden thought striking him, "you baked the birthday cake last year."

Joseph laughed. "No. Not me. Harmony did when I told her when your birthday was. I simply made sure Augustus didn't know about it when she snuck it into your room." He slowed and waited another beat. "Morgan—"

"I don't want to go back," Morgan said.

"I know. I can't force you. No one can," Joseph said, keeping his words slow. "But you *are* Blackburn's Divine and Morgan both. Solitude is yours and yours alone to do with whatever you choose, but *please*."

He wanted Morgan to return. The dead in Blackburn relied on him. He had a sacred job, one he hadn't been able to ignore on the trip even if it had been his intent. The girl and the dead souls were proof of that. They alone reminded him of what he was. Not just Morgan, but also the Divine.

Morgan sighed, long and slow, and it shook as it came out. Silent tears slid down his cheeks. Relief at one turn, but right back to desolation at the next. He buried his face against his knees and covered his head with his arms. Just so he didn't have to look at Joseph's expecting face. Make a damn decision he couldn't. Not now. His fingers had just begun to curl up in his hair when warm hands stopped them.

"Morgan," Joseph whispered, this time much closer as he gently drew Morgan's arms away from his head. "I'm sorry."

It really sounded like he was.

"I'll go back," Morgan whispered, so quietly he barely heard himself. "Just not right now. Give me more time."

Joseph was smiling sadly when Morgan chanced looking at him. "You still have your solitude," he said, gently rubbing a thumb over one of the bruises along Morgan's arm. "The Autumnal Equinox service is very soon, so this is as far as Augustus will go. I don't know what he intends to do afterward other than get Rosenburg authorities involved for a wider search." He gave Morgan a sad smile. "But please, take this time to be the person we stole from you. Be Morgan."

He stood without waiting for a real promise, straightening his cassock as he went. Though Morgan saw his lips move, like he wanted to say goodbye, he didn't. Because he wanted to believe it really wasn't goodbye and Morgan couldn't assure him whether he was right or not. He slipped around the tree and Morgan silently let him go.

It wasn't long before whispers between Joseph and Harmony floated above the silence, but then they were walking away. Part of Morgan knew he should have looked around the tree, just to see Harmony again to memorize her face, but he stayed rooted in place. She hadn't come to see him either; maybe she was afraid it would weaken her resolve to let him choose. Like it would weaken his own resolve if he watched them.

Not watching made it easier to let them go because he didn't know if he wanted to keep his promise.

He stayed where he was, listening intently to the grove around him. The hushed silence returned, like no one had ever intruded, and Morgan closed his eyes. It was peace, in a way. Too early for cars on the distant road, too late for night critters—not that they'd be around with Morgan invading their space—and, for once, his thoughts were a quiet, gentle buzz. Not the overwhelming wave they'd always been. He was himself within the grove of pines.

Reality crashed back when new footsteps hurried around the trees, leaving Morgan panicked again. He still didn't know *where* he was and now someone else was here. He jerked away from the tree, intending to run, but he'd barely gotten up before a hand caught his arm. Fin's hand. It wasted no time pulling Morgan into a tight hug and Morgan could have collapsed from relief if Fin wasn't keeping him upright.

"Thank the Lady," he breathed. "I was worried you'd gone too far."

"I'm fine," Morgan said, gently resting his head against Fin. Part of him wanted to stay like this for as long as he could, but then Fin stepped back to hold him at an arm's length. "Is Eryn okay?"

Fin's hands lingered on Morgan's shoulders like he feared he'd lose Morgan otherwise. "She's fine," he said. "That prick of a prior was tearing up the room while she watched and then apparently Vesper and Aurora walked by?" He laughed, still winded, and it bubbled out of his throat like he hadn't meant to. "Augustus turned just in time to see that guy's white hair and the audacity, right? While he was distracted, Eryn sneaked out and by then I was back." He released Morgan, like he just realized he was still holding him, and crossed his arms. "Eryn's keeping a look out with the car. S-So you climbed all on your own, then?"

Morgan nodded and his stomach flipped when Fin beamed at him like everything was right with the world. It *was* the smile he knew; the one he'd once memorized—he was so sure of it now. "Like it was hard," Morgan teased and Fin's grin grew wider.

Superficial words brushing aside what Morgan wanted to say and didn't know how. The words jumbled together in his head, vanishing in his throat, and he lost all his nerve. What did it matter if he was going to return and become the Divine once more? It might only hurt Fin even more.

Except at the same time, he couldn't ignore how he felt toward Fin. Couldn't accept losing all those memories that were his alone. The indecision snared him still like he was caught in a trap.

"There's a diner nearby," Fin said, interrupting Morgan's spiral of thoughts, and Fin nodded toward the way he'd come. "Gas station wraps were *not* looking good for breakfast. My grandma liked this place. Real food." He paused and watched Morgan, concerned. "Morgan? Are-Are you all right?"

"Yes," Morgan forced the word out of his throat. "I am hungry, though. A-And please." There was a question hanging in the air even if Fin didn't outright say it. "Don't let them ruin our road trip. I still want to go to everything."

Fin closed his mouth, worry fading into warmth. He grinned, wide and true. "Priory's never stopped me before." He winked and held out his hand. "And it won't now. Come on. Eryn's waiting."

Even as the unease of the promise grew in his stomach, becoming a lump of dread, Morgan smiled too, taking Fin's hand tightly. The priory wouldn't ruin his life. Not a second time.

XII.
Memories of the Fair

The diner was just down the road and on the drive over, Eryn gleefully told Morgan all about how frustrated the Head Prior had been when he didn't find Morgan at all. Truth be told, Morgan would have loved to have seen the smugness wiped off his face, but he had to make do with imagining it on his own. Eryn's description certainly helped.

The diner's red roof shimmered bright against the still rising sun when they arrived and the smell of freshly brewed coffee wafted out of the sliding doors as they stepped inside. Morgan couldn't help but breathe it in deep; it reminded him of *something*, but that something was too fuzzy to grasp. Not many people lingered inside yet, just a small line of truckers drinking their morning coffee at the front bar and, of course, Vesper and Aurora sat at a booth at the far end.

Even though Morgan felt he owed Vesper a thank you for distracting the Head Prior, he decided a nod would do while Eryn pulled him and Fin into a booth at the other end so they could order.

Eryn ordered a concoction of pancakes merged with a cinnamon swirl bun all covered in white icing. Way more sugar than Morgan had ever seen on one plate. Especially once she'd taken it upon herself to drizzle copious amounts of syrup atop the berries it had also come with. Fin ordered what the waitress called a stuffed eggy bread—it was two slices of bread toasted in a batter made of eggs and sandwiched between them was cream cheese, strawberries, and banana slices. Morgan felt a little boring with his apple cinnamon oatmeal when everything came out, but Eryn and Fin happily fed him pieces of their breakfasts to make up for it.

The ease was nice after how fraught everything had been before from the nightmare, to his conversation with Fin, and then to the Head Prior almost catching him. Maybe it was the sugar talking, but Morgan began to feel much more energized.

Energy making him bolder, he thought once again to ask Fin all the questions swirling in his mind, but fear kept him silent. Not today. He didn't want to ruin it any more than it already had been with fuzzy trivialities. The memories would be there tomorrow.

He hoped.

They finished eating, shared a small cup of coffee, and were on their way. The fair wasn't very far from the diner and on the way over, Fin and Eryn traded stories back and forth about their own adventures there when they were younger. According to Eryn, the fair came every autumnal equinox as a send-off for summer, while the bonfire had originated from those who wandered away from the fair, looking for something quieter by the end of the night.

Fin parked alongside other cars at the overlook between the fairgrounds and the path to the beach below and they walked the rest of the way.

Morgan kept Fin's hood securely over the hat over his hair and with the sunglasses Eryn had given him, he doubted anyone would notice he was at all Divine. Eryn even had a story ready if anyone asked why he was so covered up. Sensitive to the sun. Morgan was definitely pale enough to be and he didn't quite want to chance if it was true or not either way. Fin and Eryn, meanwhile, were still in their regular clothes, but Eryn had packed their swimsuits into the tote she carried for whenever they were ready to change. She insisted there were always public changing rooms they could use on the way down.

By the time they arrived, it was closing in on noon and a small crowd already mingled through the open attractions. There wasn't a loud thrum of excitement, at least; it was sleepy and calm. Morgan liked it, but stayed near Fin and Eryn to avoid looking at anyone outright. He'd done the same so often at the priory, it was almost second nature.

No matter what kind of sermon he had to be present for, he'd have to avoid looking at anyone because the act alone *always* caught someone's eye and invited them to try and talk to him later. He supposed he couldn't blame them; all they wanted was a connection to their Divine, but he always felt bad he couldn't give them one. Many times, he'd stayed near the Head Prior after sermons because if anyone came to talk to him, they'd inevitably end up talking to the Head Prior instead because of his arrogance. It was perhaps the only good thing he'd ever done for Morgan and Morgan doubted he ever realized it.

Thinking of the Head Prior at all made Morgan alert and he glanced around to make sure he wasn't actually in the crowd. No dark cassocks shadowing them as far as he could see. Just all sorts of different people absorbed in their own lives. Maybe Joseph was right; the Head Prior must have gone back to Blackburn once he'd lost the trail. And, with the Head Prior's hesitation of telling people Morgan was missing, no one would be on the lookout for a runaway Divine. Maybe Morgan was really free. The warm thought settled inside him, making him tingly, and eased his worries.

"Try this!" Eryn's voice crashed through his thoughts and he jumped as she shoved something pink and fluffy at him. It was huge, almost the size of his head, and spun around a paper cone. They'd stopped at one of the food stalls where the seller was spinning another treat in his stand as a child watched, captivated at whatever the pink substance was.

"It's cotton candy," Eryn explained. She laughed when all Morgan did was stare dubiously at it.

"You eat it." Fin reached over to take a small piece. It was wispy as he drew it away and plopped it in his mouth. Eryn demonstrated too, taking some for herself.

Morgan gingerly followed their lead—their chosen breakfasts hadn't been *that* bad; maybe this would be fine too—and took a small pinch for himself. He could barely feel it, but somehow knew his fingers would be sticky afterward, and put it in his mouth.

Sugar. Just sugar. It melted on his tongue and wasn't altogether bad. Just different. Almost transient as far as food went. He tried another bite to reaffirm his opinion and it didn't change.

Fin forced back a laugh before he spoke. "That's the same expression he made with the soda!"

Morgan's face warmed and Eryn huffed. "They never let you have anything good at the priory, huh?" She took a big handful for herself and stuffed it into her mouth.

Morgan tried to laugh it away, feeling some of his nerves edge back. "Not like this."

Eryn's eyes lit up and she faced Fin who'd taken another mouthful of cotton candy. "We should try a corn dog!"

Morgan lost track of time as they went up and down the food stalls trying every little treat. None of them really felt *right*, but he was glad Fin and Eryn weren't altogether disappointed when he didn't like them as much as they did. They found it funny. Corndog was all right, candy apple not enjoyable, something sweet and creamy deep-fried and crunchy that he did not want to eat again, and so many more snacks he hardly had a chance to look at before he took a bite and decided never again.

Once their food adventures were over, Eryn dragged them to the rides. There weren't many lines yet, at least, and the first one they chose, Morgan didn't even catch the name before Fin and Eryn were dragging him into the seat to sit between them. Eryn had left her tote bag with the ride operator (it was a sad lump at his feet) and before Morgan could ask her why—and also why she took off his sunglasses and stuffed them into her pocket—the bar came down over their laps and the ride lifted them into the air.

In seconds, the world spun too fast for Morgan to keep up.

Colors blurred into continuous streaks as screams of delights filled Morgan's ears while Fin and Eryn's own laughter grounded him as much as it could. Morgan had to squeeze his eyes shut anyway just to make the colors stop. It was exhilarating, no doubt about it, stealing all of his thoughts away as they spun around and around with everyone else. It ended soon enough, and though Fin and Eryn could walk a straight line afterward, Morgan couldn't. His legs shook, his stomach threatened to revolt, and as Eryn took his hand to pull him toward another ride—another spinning one at a glance—Fin stopped her.

"Morgan?" he said and since none of them were moving—except in Morgan's vision—Morgan took the chance to bend over, hands on his knees. Even the ground felt like it was spinning. Fin started and put a warm hand at his back. "Hey—hey, are you okay?"

Morgan tried to laugh it off, but all he managed was a weak sound and shook his head. Fin rubbed gentle circles across his back. Morgan took deep breaths; he was *not* going to vomit and ruin their day. "Everything's still spinning," he managed to squeeze out. "No more rides like that."

He hated admitting defeat. Fin and Eryn must have ridden a dozen or more throughout the years, coming out unscathed, and he'd been done in by one.

"I should have started with bumper cars," Eryn said, palming her forehead. "Something quiet... let me see." She stood on her tiptoes and scanned the fairground. She squeaked, batting her hand toward Fin until he helped Morgan steady himself upright. "I got one! How are you with heights, Morgan?"

Morgan's thoughts flew back to his escape from the priory. Instead of the sickening churn like he expected, his stomach made butterflies instead. He thought of the pine tree, but he hadn't really seen *how* high he'd been; there had been too much blocking his view.

He drew his gaze after Eryn's and caught what she was looking at: the giant wheel standing against the horizon at the end of the fairground. Aptly named, the wheel was large and held onto little swaying gondolas as the entire thing slowly turned.

He must have stared at it too long, drinking in the sight, as Fin's hand returned to his back. Thoughts settled and slowed, making Morgan altogether warm.

"Yes," he said. "Let's do that one."

The wheel had a line—Eryn said it always did—but Morgan didn't mind waiting and watched the crowds. There were families, the elderly, children squirming in place, couples holding hands—a sampling of all sorts of people. The crowds had steadily grown around them as the afternoon wore on and he was glad everyone stayed lost in their own worlds.

As he drew his gaze back to the wheel, he caught a flash of white hair in the crowd disembarking from the ride.

Vesper and Aurora were coming toward them and Morgan's entire body tingled as he watched them. He quickly looked away as they drew closer, trying not to be noticed himself, but Vesper glanced up at them anyway. Aurora smiled warmly and waved.

"Fancy meeting you three here," she said as they stopped beside them. She wore a floral summer dress this time, full of pinks and oranges, and a wide-brim hat with a bow on the back. "You could have sat with us at the diner! We wouldn't have minded. How are you guys enjoying the fair so far?"

Eryn eyed her suspiciously, but in a teasing way. "I think you're following us!"

Aurora grinned at her, propping her hands on her hips as Vesper shook his head, chuckling. "We got here first, missy! If anyone's following anyone, it's you guys!" She winked and she and Eryn devolved into a shared giggle. As it tapered off, she gazed at them one by one, like committing them to memory. The warmth Morgan had felt last night returned as a wave. Like arms wanted to wrap him up again and keep him warm. "You going to the bonfire later?"

Fin shrugged, one hand touching Eryn's as she opened her mouth. "Maybe," he said. "Eryn, the line's moving."

Eryn gave Aurora and Vesper a quick wave. "See you around!"

Fin shuffled them forward together and Aurora and Vesper went on their way. Morgan chanced a glance over his shoulder as they went and noticed Vesper quickly looking away as though he'd been caught staring. No—he hadn't been. Morgan's mind was making it up, just like it made up they were familiar somehow. He would have remembered someone with dyed white hair coming to the priory. It would have been a hot topic and no one would have stopped talking about it.

And yet, no one else gave him a second glance. Like it was somehow normal outside the walls of the priory. Maybe no one but the very devout even cared.

"Sorry," Eryn mumbled once they were far enough away. "Aurora's face just makes me want to talk to her. And you know, I keep thinking Vesper and Aurora walked by when they did at the motel *on purpose*. Their room was clear on the other side—there was no reason to even come near our door."

Fin shook his head. "I don't mean you shouldn't talk to them. It's just... them just running into us constantly creeps me out. I don't know why." He peered over his shoulder, but the couple was gone beyond the crowd.

"This is a popular destination now," Eryn said. "We could just be biased since we saw them once already. So, in a way, we're just looking out for one another since they're now familiar faces."

She wasn't wrong, but Morgan didn't want to think about it anymore; it'd simply undo his day of enjoying everything the fair had. They'd come to the front of the line, at least, and the attendant was letting another group out of the gondola waiting for them.

Eryn straightened suddenly and faced Fin with a sly smile. "You want to take him up?" Fin's eyebrows shot up. "I can watch from here—heights are a little scary."

Morgan's body buzzed as he realized what she was doing. Giving them time to talk. Alone. They'd have all the time in the world on a ride taking them into the sky as slowly as it moved. At the same time, however, he *still* didn't know how to raise the subject. If it went wrong, they'd be stuck in the air.

"Hey—come on." Fin laughed weakly. "You love this ride, Eryn. You aren't scared of heights." His voice had an edge of panic to it, but he covered it with another short laugh. It reminded Morgan of Fin's reaction after kissing his cheek.

Perhaps it hadn't been a fully conscious choice then. It explained his sudden panic and escape afterward under the guise of getting breakfast. Why even he didn't bring it up after the Head Prior had been dealt with. Whatever the kiss was, it had been a reflex. Maybe something he'd done before.

Eryn made a face. "Okay, *fine*."

"Are you three getting on or what?" the attendant interrupted with a tired look.

"I'm going, I'm going!" Eryn quickly slid aboard and Fin ushered Morgan and himself on after her.

The gondola was made of wood and painted a garish color—theirs was red, but the others around them varied from yellow, blue, and then red again—and had seats facing one another while it remained open at the sides. The top reminded Morgan of a tent and metal rods kept it attached to the gondola below.

Eryn positioned herself in the middle on one side, leaving Fin and Morgan to sit together on the other. Someone had carved their initials into the bench and as Morgan grazed his hand over it, he felt a gentle tug of memory. He let it go when the ride attendant secured the metal bar across their laps and muttered all the safety rules—keep all limbs safely inside the gondola and don't stand while the ride is in motion—before he left.

The wheel vibrated as they lifted off the ground, but they didn't rise far; as soon as the next gondola was in front of the ride attendant, they stopped in place.

"It's normal," Fin said as Morgan held onto the metal bar. "They're still loading everyone."

"Oh." Morgan relaxed and tilted his head back. There were so many gondolas following the wheel above them. "Is this it then? Starting and stopping?"

Eryn giggled. "You're the one who wanted nothing fast!" She playfully kicked her feet at Morgan. He nudged her back, barely hiding the chuckle in his throat, and Fin joined in. Between the three of them, it made their gondola swing back and forth until another ride attendant told them to quit it. "It'll do this until it has a whole new crew of people onboard then we have at least two full rotations. It's smooth once we really get going, don't worry."

Fin nodded and stretched his arms across the back of the gondola, one behind Morgan. "This was my grandma's favorite ride," he said, looking out as the wheel turned again, taking them higher. "She liked the peacefulness. Always took photos too that she used as reference for paintings later."

Just thinking about her ignited memories in Morgan's thoughts. Sitting in a similar gondola with Fin on her lap, and then with Fin on one side, a little more grown, and a little Eryn on her other side. More memories eagerly joined Beatrice's; all sorts of different lives coming into the gondola with friends, families, partners, to just be whisked away into the sky. He let them go shortly after they surfaced, reminding himself to be Morgan—not the Divine.

It was a few more stops and starts before the wheel turned its full circle at a leisurely pace. Like Eryn said, it was smooth with a gentle sway in the breeze. They drew high into the air and Morgan breathed in deep.

There it was; the last breath of summer rustling

over them, bringing with it air smelling of autumn. The view from the top let him see the early trees medleys of reds and oranges peeking out from the sea of green trees.

"I like it up here too," Fin said and Morgan realized Fin had been watching him. "What's your favorite season?"

"Autumn," Morgan said without hesitation. "I like the way the trees change." The gondola began its descent and he lost sight of the trees the lower they went. "It makes me feel cozy at the priory too. I wear my heavier robes and they bring in more blankets. Sometimes hot cider during dinner." He huddled himself further into Fin's jacket, wrapping it tighter. "It's nice."

Eryn nodded and leaned back. "I like autumn too," she said. "It always feels like it signifies change." She gently nudged Fin's foot and then Morgan's. "And I guess it does. Lots of things end with autumn and others begin."

"Like school," Fin said, casting his gaze away from her.

She'd be going away soon and now, because she was a friend, it left Morgan uneasy. Even she looked sad thinking about it. It only lasted a moment, however; she slapped her cheeks and grinned at them.

"We should sneak you some fresh apple cider," Eryn said. "I bet I can get away from school for a day trip." She nudged Fin again and he nodded, grinning. "Fin's grandma always took us to this cider mill past Rosenburg that hosted apple picking tours. She'd pick up this huge jug of apple cider they make in-house to take home. It'd take *weeks* to finish it off with just Fin and his grandma, but I always came over to help."

Even though she'd smiled as she spoke, her voice turned sad, like the universe was reminding her Beatrice could no longer take them anywhere. Even Fin's smile dropped and he'd gone back to looking distantly off the side. Change had already happened and would happen still. Beatrice had passed away and Eryn was leaving Fin in Blackburn. Morgan wasn't sure what he'd do yet. All he knew right now was he wanted to make them feel better, but had no idea what to say. He stayed quiet in the end, a silent reverence at least for Beatrice's memory. Soon enough, Eryn snapped out of her thoughts and filled their silence with everything she could see as they rose into the sky again.

By the time their gondola came back down and they disembarked, the uneasy silence had melted, and Fin and Eryn shot ideas back and forth about what to do next. The crowds had grown even larger while they'd been up in the air and being so close to so many people made Morgan's skin prickle with nerves.

Fin took them over to the game stalls, away from the crowds surging to get on the rides, and the first one he chose was simple: throw rings and score a prize if the ring landed on the correct peg. Morgan was pretty bad at it. Each of his rings missed their mark completely, not even close. Eryn wouldn't try, but Fin was determined to win *something*. Morgan liked watching him; the way his mouth tightened in concentration was cute. He had a deftness to his throws, even if the rings still pinged off their mark.

A group passed them, drawing Morgan's attention. It was a mother and father, a little girl balanced on her father's shoulders while an older boy held onto the mother's hand. They blended in with everyone, incredibly nondescript with nothing Morgan could use to recognize them later, but his gaze lingered.

Memories itched back into focus, clawing over reality to be noticed again. They were from something long gone, out of reach. Black hair draped in sunflower petals in the mirror. Then seeing the world so high atop his father's shoulders. A face he couldn't remember. A name gone to the throes of memories not his own. His mother smiled at him, even if all he knew was that she smiled—not what she looked like. She had a sunflower behind her ear. No—she didn't. It was the little girl running through the crowds, holding his hand. Then there was an old couple leaning into one another, hands clasped together, as they sat in the gondola, rising higher in the sky as it grew big and wide.

Everything around him was too steeped in memories. They all wanted to be seen at once, as though just realizing *what* he was. He couldn't hide from the sensation. Rising from the memories was a soft chorus of voices, speaking about their lives and the hum touched each stall, each ride, all across the entire fair. It was too much. They wanted a witness for their memories. All the ones buried beneath fairs long past, ones attached to names he'd already sent, and even the girl who'd barely lived. He wanted the calm silence back. Just him and the trees. Not this onslaught.

The air grew cold, a shimmer to it that it didn't have before, reminding him of the nightmare. The fire came next, as it always did. A denial of himself, eating up the memories so all he could think of was the fire he should never have internalized. The flames were bright against the rides, against the stalls, everywhere.

"Morgan?"

His name echoed distantly. The warm hand was at his back again, ripping him away from the memories begging to be remembered and from the flames swallowing him up. Morgan snapped his eyes open, reality returning in such stark focus, it made him dizzy. Fin and Eryn were in front of him, worried.

Morgan eased in a breath. *I am Morgan*, he told himself. *I am with Fin and Eryn—my friends.*

"Hey," Fin whispered, his voice soothing. They'd drawn Morgan away from the crowds and stood shadowed between two stalls. Fairgoers continued back and forth around them, but no one else noticed Morgan's panic.

Fin gently pushed a lock of hair back into the hood, making Morgan's skin flush as they touched, and he finally looked up at Fin. "What's wrong?"

Morgan shook his head, his breathing coming out in shallow bursts like he was starved for air. "It's too much," he whispered, sad he had to admit it at all. "There's so many memories."

Eryn's eyebrows knitted together in worry. "It's okay," she said. "It's beach time anyway!" Her entire presence warmed and Morgan was so glad for her exuberance. "Everyone's here now, so it's the perfect time to head out. Good way to cool off too." She nudged Fin with her elbow. "Fin also won you something, by the way."

Morgan finally noticed the plush rabbit in Fin's arm. It was speckled brown, floppy, and had a little red scarf. Fin handed it over, smiling.

"Now you have one of your own," Fin said. "Not one I've ever drooled on."

Eryn laughed suddenly, clapping her hands over her mouth to try to smother it, and Fin gave her a tired look, playfully shoving her shoulder. Morgan hardly registered them; his eyes were glued to the rabbit. *His* rabbit. He gently pressed it close to his chest.

"Thank you," he said. "I love it."

His and his alone. The priory wouldn't take it away like they had every other asset of his life; he wouldn't allow it.

Fin and Eryn pressed Morgan between themselves and together, the three of them escaped the growing crowds. At the outskirts, near the path they'd taken to come in, was another trail leading away and Eryn steered them toward it. There was a small rest area at the end and she and Fin agreed to get changed. Since Morgan had nothing to change into of his own, he opted to remain outside to wait for them and held onto Eryn's tote with his stuffed rabbit safely nestled inside.

The rest area was empty aside from him and he

was glad for it. The fair had become a soft echo past the trees instead of the onslaught of noise. Much better.

Being alone, however, left him nervous. He wished he'd gone in with Fin. Then again, watching him change, even being close to him as he did so, would have probably flustered Morgan too much. His heart was already racing just thinking about it, remembering the way Fin was that morning, the muscles along his back Morgan still so badly wanted to trace...

Morgan shook his head, trying to ignore the thoughts coursing warmth throughout every limb. All he was doing was making himself flustered; he had to stop. Fin would be out soon. He'd be fine.

"Hey you."

Morgan jumped, hearing the low voice so close to him, and he turned. Vesper stood beside him and Morgan couldn't help it when his jaw dropped. There was no way Morgan had been so deep in his thoughts he simply didn't hear Vesper approach. The world shifted with his presence so close, becoming fuzzy and unreal at the edges, but Vesper somehow remained clear. His gray eyes locked with Morgan's and he tilted his head.

"Waiting for your friends?" he asked. "Aurora's in there too. She suddenly decided it was swim time."

Morgan drew himself tighter, taking a step away. Some of the world cleared, reality locking into place once more. "You aren't going to swim with her?"

"Forgot my swimwear," Vesper said. He hadn't taken his gaze away. Morgan knew *he* should have turned, but he felt trapped in the man's soft gray eyes. Vesper opened his mouth to speak again, but shut it just as fast and looked away finally, releasing Morgan from whatever spell he'd had him under.

"Hey!" came Fin's voice, pulling Morgan fully back to reality. He'd emerged and stood at Morgan's other side, dressed in his black swim trunks and a red woven button-up. He gently stepped between Morgan and Vesper and settled a hard look on the man. "Something wrong?"

Vesper studied him up and down before looking away completely. "Waiting for my wife. Is that a problem?"

Fin narrowed his eyes, his shoulders tensing. "N-No. It's not."

The silence that followed was heavy. Fin didn't stop watching Vesper, even though Vesper wouldn't meet the challenge, and Morgan stayed behind Fin. Thankfully, the stalemate melted when Vesper's lips shifted into a smile, his entire posture relaxing. Aurora came out of the other side of the changing rooms, shuffling a flustered Eryn with her.

Morgan instantly understood *why* she was flustered; Aurora had changed into a white two-piece swimsuit, showcasing her glowing skin and ample curves, and had a sheer shawl thrown over that. Somehow, the shawl shimmered and she looked like sunshine incarnate. Eryn's swimsuit was quaint by comparison; a teal one-piece with a colorful shawl draped across her shoulders and kept cinched at the waist with a red tie.

"Sorry for the wait," Aurora said, a spring to her step as she came up to Vesper. She pecked him on the cheek and beamed at Morgan and Fin. "Did you three want to walk with us? I know this cute ice cream place on the way."

"No, we're fine." Fin awkwardly met her smile. "Enjoy yourselves."

Vesper eyed him for another moment before he slid an arm around Aurora's back and held her closer. "All right then," he said slowly. "See you around."

Once they were far enough away, Eryn released a long sigh. "I am so sorry I took so long," she said. "I finished changing and then when I came out—bam! There Aurora was having trouble tying her top." She buried her face in her hands, cheeks blooming red. "No one should be that hot."

"I didn't even hear Vesper walk up," Morgan said as he helped Fin and Eryn cram their folded clothes into the tote.

Eryn nodded. "I didn't even know anyone else was in there until I came out of the stall." She chewed on her lip, looking down the path Vesper and Aurora walked. They were leaning into one another as they went. "Although, I could have been distracted."

Fin looked toward them too, frowning. "We don't have to go," he said. "We can drive somewhere else. There's tons of beaches around here."

Morgan shook his head quickly. "I want to go to the bonfire," he said. "It's why we came. It might be the last time I can. Their weirdness won't ruin it."

Though Fin and Eryn shared a look, reminiscent of the one they shared back at Fin's house, they ended it smiling at Morgan. Fin drew him closer, one arm around his shoulder, and Eryn did the same on his other side.

"Then let's get going," Fin said. "Day's wasting away and I want to swim."

XIII.
Summer's End

By mid-afternoon, they'd made a pit stop at Fin's car to grab the cooler and the other tote with the blankets and towels, and then headed down the incline. The beach itself was nestled in a small cove, making it feel intimate and close. When they came down, the view left Morgan speechless and Fin and Eryn let him take it all in without breaking the silence.

The skies remained their brilliant blue, hardly a cloud above them, and allowed the sunlight to glitter bright across the waves slowly moving to and from the sandy shore in elegant motions. Remnants of another bonfire lingered up the shore, ash and soot buried across the sand. A small group had already arrived and was bringing in piles of wood to start it anew, but otherwise, there weren't many on the beach yet and no one looked their way.

Fin and Eryn chose a shaded spot on the grass nearby and spread one of the blankets across it. The cooler and their shoes claimed it as theirs and Eryn went digging for her sunscreen.

As Fin took off the red button-up he'd been wearing, Morgan trailed his gaze away so he wasn't caught looking—he'd seen Fin shirtless already; this shouldn't have flustered him—and suddenly found himself worried about his borrowed clothes.

"W-Wait," Morgan said and Eryn lifted her head. "I shouldn't get these wet."

Eryn rolled her eyes and flapped a hand at him. "Clothes can dry!" She extracted her sunscreen and beckoned him and Fin closer. "Another chance to frolic in the waves like this isn't gonna happen again. Come on. Sunscreen time!"

At the very least, Morgan left Fin's jacket folded neatly with their things. Eryn slapped copious amounts of sunscreen on the three of them as quickly as she could, taking care to make sure Morgan was covered in the stuff twice over—it smelled pleasantly of coconut, thankfully—and hurried them into the water with her.

The fair had distracted Morgan from the bruises still stark on his arms and he only noticed them again when they were running toward the water. There was the kneejerk reaction to rush back for the coat to hide them, but Morgan kept running with Fin and Eryn instead. He wouldn't let anything ruin this. It helped Fin and Eryn didn't look at them and only urged him on with large smiles.

Against Morgan's bare feet, the water was cool and the ground coarse, but it was real. Part of the world. He would have been happy staying put, merely ankle deep, but it didn't take long for Fin and Eryn to tire of splashing each other and they pulled him farther until they were waist deep.

While they debated how best to teach him, Morgan focused on the ripples the three of them made, the sound the wind sung as it blew across the water, and the soft chatter from farther down the beach. After how packed the fair was, the quiet chatter was a calming respite. Morgan only hoped it stayed that way.

Fin and Eryn finally decided to start with the basics: floating. Morgan had been uneasy about letting both feet leave the ground, but Fin promised he wouldn't let Morgan sink. Propping his arm securely around Morgan's back, he and Eryn helped Morgan lay horizontal in the water and once he was set, Eryn moved away and let Fin handle it. Fin kept his hands gently nearby, giving Morgan the ghost of a push if he dipped too far or needed reassurance he was doing fine. As long as Fin stayed right there, Morgan figured he could do it. Eryn floated beside him before long, showing him how easy it was supposed to be, and he resisted the urge to splash her.

It was nice, though; floating in the water was, in a way, surreal. The world was simply there, not dragging him every which way for his attention like the fair and everything else, and he could simply be. His breathing was slow, relaxed, and he wouldn't have minded staying there all day. All night. Watch the sky go from blue to purple to black until a wash of stars glittered above them.

He was so deep in his thoughts, he'd hardly realized Fin had moved his hands until Fin was floating beside him.

The prospect of sinking shredded all his relaxation and Morgan did the first thing that came naturally to his panicked mind: thrashed and searched for ground. Fin and Eryn righted him before he swallowed any water at least, and were trying not to laugh as he caught his breath.

"Sorry," Morgan said, hardly containing laughter himself.

Fin snickered. "I've been elbowed harder, believe me."

The chatter on the beach was closer now; others

continued to arrive, setting up places to sit around the up-and-coming bonfire. Children were nearby, splashing each other while their parents watched from the shore. Morgan caught sight of Aurora further up the beach, swimming parallel to the shore and Vesper strolled after her, the sheer shawl draped over his arm and her sandals strapped across his hand. No one looked at them but Morgan, like somehow, they didn't exist until Morgan was there to acknowledge them.

Morgan shook his head; the thought was silly. It was simply what Eryn had said earlier: they had a chance meeting and now easily recognized each other since they were familiar faces. He ignored them. No more weirdness. He wanted to focus on the remainder of the day. Enjoy it while it lasted.

Fin gently placed his hands on Morgan's waist—the act alone racing butterflies up Morgan's stomach—but all he did was direct Morgan on how to float again. Before he got too far, however, a few of the splashing children had ceased playing and were coming closer.

Fin snorted. "Eryn, I bet those are the kids you played with last time."

Eryn peered over, shielding her eyes from the sun. She laughed. "You're right!" She waved and the kids practically shoved past one another to return it.

"Hey!" She waded toward them, pointing at the shallow end of the beach. "This is too deep! Back! You're too short!"

Morgan looked up at Fin; he hadn't let go of Morgan's waist, but he was watching Eryn fondly, like he wanted to join her.

"You can go with them," Morgan said. "I want to dry off. I'm getting cold."

Fin blinked and stared at Morgan. "You sure?"

Morgan nodded; he *was* a little cold. It wasn't a lie born out of anxiety, at least not entirely. "If I wasn't with you, you would have." He extracted himself from Fin and squeezed his hands. "I promise I'll be fine. I just want to watch for a little bit."

The earlier freedom had come and gone. Too many people were around him and it was only a matter of time before they realized he didn't just have blond hair that looked white peeking out of his hat. The seenness itched into him like a maligned thought, worse than what he'd felt at the fair, and he wanted to squash it before it grew. Sitting and watching, just being Morgan would be enough, he was sure.

He was glad when Fin relented and helped him back to the beach.

The spot where they'd left their belongings was still uncrowded, thankfully. The shade from the nearby tree was a welcome respite from the sun and Morgan felt instantly better as he dried off. He stripped the still wet hat from his head, wringing it out, and hid himself beneath Fin's dry jacket.

Fin was digging in his tote as Morgan settled down and brought out his camera. He fidgeted with a moment before gently handing it over. "Probably should have had this at the fair, but feel free to take some pictures now. More memories, right?" He smiled softly. "I don't want you to forget anything."

Morgan nodded, holding the camera close, and watched Fin returned to the waves where the children were chanting his name. Morgan gingerly raised the camera, centered Fin in the viewfinder, and snapped his first photo all on his own. It came out pretty decent, all things considered. It wasn't too crooked and Fin was in the center as the sun lit him up like gold. Definitely one to keep. Morgan settled it beside him and noticed Fin glancing back at him, worried. He met Fin's concern with a smile and a small wave. It was enough to help Fin let go of what-ever had worried him and he faced the children with a large grin.

It was soothing watching Fin be himself while he splashed Eryn and let the children drag him this way and that. Somehow freer. He'd been gentle and kind to Morgan, but there was always some restraint he didn't have now. His smile was wider, as free as he acted, like he'd ceased thinking so hard about whatever it was, especially as he threw the older kids further into the water. They'd always come back immediately, laughing, for another toss Fin was sure to give them.

Morgan tried not to think so hard about it and watched the younger children instead. When they weren't cheering Fin on, they stuck near Eryn as they searched the shallow water for shells. Morgan got a few shots of them too, but they came out blurrier than he'd intended.

As the day wore on and the sun began its descent from the sky, more groups arrived, many Morgan was sure he recognized from the fair. The bonfire was stacked high with wood, but still remained unlit. Grills were set up nearby, the smell of food beginning to waft over, but Morgan wasn't hungry yet.

A few children seemed curious about him, but their parents helpfully kept them away. The only ones who fully made the trek over were those who'd been with Eryn. They brought him seashells of all kinds, their unsure expressions melting into smiles when he thanked them, and then they'd run back to find more. He wasn't sure what brought it on, but soon he had quite the collection. He even made sure to immortalize it in another photo. Just in case he couldn't keep them.

That the children thought of him at all made him feel less lonely. Something he hadn't even realized he'd been feeling until the children entrusted him with the shells. Morgan told himself he could just rejoin Fin and Eryn, but he worried ruining their day by being noticed and he hated it.

At least the seashells were nice.

They were smooth underneath his fingertips. Pale and bleached, but each one still had a slight ribbon of color coating the inside. As he examined them closely, subtle hums traced his fingertips. Tiny memories of lives that had grazed the shells long before. Glimpses at most, nothing concrete or wrong, just evidence of life.

It was softer than the fair had been. Not an overwhelming wave crashing into him, but little trickles. Maybe the whole world was like the shells and the fair and he'd just never noticed. The priory, while alive with activity from the clergy, felt like a tomb in retrospect. Memories were scrubbed clean so he could do his duty unhindered.

The books Felicity had brought him had been like the shells. Countless lives grazing the spines, reading the pages, and each life had melded into the next that happened across it. Maybe standing inside the library would feel the same. Microcosms of life.

It was all memories in the end. The uniqueness of each life walking the world boiled down to glimpses that held no reference once they were filtered through the Divine. His were the same. They'd been filtered out long ago, leaving but glimpses at most. If what he'd seen before was even his. He lifted his gaze to watch the waves; they reminded him of his own memories ebbing out of reach.

He couldn't remember his mother's name any longer. Sleep and adventure had taken it far away, but perhaps it hadn't really been her name. Just like he'd ascribed a new name to his father somewhere down the line, he'd likely done the same with her.

No. He would not dwell on a life he'd never have again.

He had one now, or something like it. He watched Fin and traced his body with his eyes. The curve of his nose against the setting sun. The way his lips moved as he spoke. Every bit of Fin lighted something inside Morgan and he wished he could recall with clarity if Fin really had been his previous attendant.

Even though he swore he could feel the heat of the lips again, he still couldn't remember anything more. Not the shape of the body, the curve of the eyes, or even how tall he'd been. Besides, if his attendant was brave enough to kiss him—the

Divine—would he have really kept his cowl on at all times? Then again, Morgan's memories were faulty. Perhaps the rest of the face was simply lost behind all the other memories that weren't his.

There *had* to be more. Something to tell Morgan without a doubt it was Fin before he gathered his nerve. He concentrated harder, focusing as deep as he could on the way the kisses had made him feel, and more and more, he felt a body press against his as his own hands gripped robes to pull it closer. Physical and tangible, right there.

The ghost of a memory made Morgan flush all the way down before it fled.

Staring only brought him attention. Fin always looked concerned when he glanced back and a few times, Morgan managed to pretend he was taking a photo instead of staring to search for memories. The one time he wasn't fast enough, however, Fin took it as an invitation to come back. The freedom suddenly gone, locked away, and Morgan hated that it was because of him.

Fin hid his concern with another smile as he approached, but this one, Morgan saw the tiredness in it. Morgan placed the camera back down and hugged his knees to his chest, giving Fin room as he settled beside him.

"I think the kids will be the death of me," he said

and shivered as he quickly toweled himself off. "I don't get how Eryn keeps up. She's not even tired."

Morgan gazed back to the sea. Eryn was surrounded, kids barely reaching past her waist trying to tell her all at once how they'd been doing. There was the largest grin plastered on her lips—one much livelier than she'd had at the fair—as she considered each child fondly.

Fin shrugged on his shirt, buttoning it halfway up. "I thought it'd be quieter with everyone at the fair." He watched a small group pass them. They were on their way to greet another family on the other side of the growing bonfire. "Word just keeps getting out and it'll just be as crowded as the fair before long. I'll miss it."

"It's all right," Morgan said, thumbing the shells near his feet. Fin picked one up and inspected it. "It's been nice to watch."

Fin nodded and as he set the shell back down, his eye caught the pile of photos Morgan had taken. As he reached around to look at the photos, his smile turned warm. It was so familiar to Morgan. "These are nice!" he said, catching Morgan's attention.

"They're blurry and crooked," Morgan argued.

"Your hands just aren't steady. It takes practice." Fin returned the photos beside the shells in a neat pile and Morgan realized the smile had disappeared.

"Is... Is everything all right?" He darted his gaze to one side. "I mean. I know. Priory. Sunflower girl. Priory again... And then the fair? Everything's a lot. When you got overwhelmed, I was really worried." He rubbed the back of his neck. "I just..."

Rambling noise to cover everything between them. What had been hanging in the air since Morgan's outburst at his house. Ever since Fin had fallen into the priory. Everything afterward. Morgan gently touched the cheek Fin had kissed. Born out of a reflex that sent him hurrying away. Fin stiffened so subtly, Morgan might have missed it if he hadn't been watching for a reaction.

He had to say something now, because if he didn't, he never would.

"You worked at the priory," Morgan finally said, resting his hand on his knee. Fin went silent and didn't move. "You were my Divine attendant, weren't you?"

A soft sigh escaped Fin's throat and he pushed his hair back. "Yes... I was."

Morgan gently bit his tongue, feeling the sting of his teeth as they pressed down. He didn't want to sound mad, even as frustration bubbled to the surface. "Why didn't you tell me?" He forced himself to keep watching Fin for a reaction, but it only made his voice shake.

"You didn't remember," Fin said, haltingly. "You didn't say anything."

"That's why you *knew* where my room was; where my veil was. My *name*." Frustration etched into Morgan's tone despite his best efforts. He was madder at himself than he was at Fin; it was his own memory he'd let sink below everything else, leaving him a hazy mess. "And then—and then you acted shocked because I didn't immediately recognize you."

"Yes." Fin drew his shoulders close. "I mean, I *was* shocked I fell on you. I meant to find the window, not the weak spot on the roof." He shook his head. "Look—"

"Why—" Morgan interrupted him. "Why didn't you say something?"

"Because!" Fin jerked to face him properly, eyes pleading. "What I did was inappropriate." He made a half, exasperated laugh sounding more pained than anything else. "Like—" He leaned back, looking away, and covered his mouth. "I had you in your room—half undressed when we were caught. I shouldn't have—"

He rambled again, half-formed words instead of something coherent, like he didn't know what else to say, but Morgan had stopped listening, instead lingering on the memories coming to life in response.

The phantom touch of fingers grazed his sides, underneath where his sash would have been. It sent goosebumps across Morgan's entire body and he covered his mouth.

"What?" he said, breathless, and Fin stammered silent. "I don't—" Morgan swallowed, lowering his hand. "I don't remember that."

Fin blinked and a slow breath eased out of him. Some of the panic had left his expression. He fidgeted, bouncing his fingers off his knees, until he crossed his legs and faced Morgan completely. "What *do* you remember?"

Not enough. Ghosts at the edge of memory.

"The first time," Morgan said, taking his turn to look away from Fin. "When you kissed me through my veil." He touched his face; the image was clearer now. Fin had suddenly asked him if he'd known what being kissed felt like. Morgan remembered simply saying no. And then Fin had bent in, giving him a soft kiss. He'd withdrawn just as fast, smiling, and told Morgan: *now he knew*.

His memory. The way his heart had sped as soon as Fin leaned in, how warmth had washed through his whole body, and how he'd practically floated into his room, touching his lips. He'd thought of Fin the entire night, unable to stop smiling.

Fin nodded slowly. "I'd asked if you'd ever

smiled before as Divine, but you just stared at me, asking what for? So... I distracted you. I wanted you to smile, even if I couldn't see it."

The words echoed in Morgan's mind. He couldn't remember why he'd been sad, except the kiss had washed it away completely and lit a desire in Morgan he'd never felt before.

"The second time we were in the cemetery," Morgan continued, his voice straining. "You asked to see my teeth." He covered his mouth lightly with his fingers. "And I liked you." He glanced up at Fin to find a soft smile on his lips this time. "So, I showed you. And you kissed me again... *feeling* my teeth."

It was so much clearer now. The way the summer evening sky glittered as the sun set, the color of the leaves above them, and how still the entire burial ground had been. The clergy must have lied to Morgan; it wasn't his divine presence upsetting anyone visiting the cemetery. They simply hadn't wanted him to go back in case it was enough to reignite his memories of Fin.

"And—" Morgan shook the thoughts from his head. The warmth of Fin's lips. How hard Morgan's heart had tried to hammer its way out of his chest. The way Fin's hands felt running through his hair and how Morgan had done it to him in turn. He'd never wanted to go back inside, but they both knew they'd have to eventually. "And that was it."

It had to be. Someone simply caught them that summer evening. Except that didn't feel true. Morgan felt his cheek. There were little touches, here and there, little kisses on the cheek when no one was looking to cheer him up. Against his fingers and wrists, making Morgan smile right behind his veil. There was so much buried under everything else, still so fuzzy and out of reach beyond the ghost of memory.

Morgan still couldn't remember *when* Fin had left; just that he was gone one morning and another clergy had volunteered to be his attendant for the day, effectively taking Fin's place. Just like Felicity. They'd lied about *why* she'd left, but not her entire existence. No one had lied about Fin; they didn't have to. Morgan had simply forgotten he'd existed at all.

A great hole opened in his stomach. They'd done something to him.

"No," Fin said. "That wasn't it. There was an-other." He cleared his throat and fidgeted with one of the shells again. "It was shortly after we kissed in the cemetery. After all the little ones. It was after din-ner. I was taking you to your room to retire. The night attendant was late. I uh..." He stammered and drew his hand away from the shell. "I asked her to give me some time alone. I wanted to talk."

Morgan drew his gaze back to the shells just as Fin peeked a glance at him. "I... I remember," he whispered. He definitely remembered a night attendant not being there when Fin took him up. "You were tapping my foot during dinner." Morgan smiled at the fuzzy memory. He'd had to keep from laughing, hiding his smile in plain view behind the veil.

Fin chuckled and nudged Morgan with his foot. Morgan nudged him back, the phantom trickle of memory falling over him.

"You started it," Fin teased. "A-anyway." He cleared his throat again. "We were talking. I just... you were humming. Smiling. I could tell even with the veil. Just happy. I wanted to ask you something—I don't even remember it now—and we were at your door. You drew me in for a kiss. And then, we went into your room. I latched the door—I swore I did— and we... well..."

Blush crept up Morgan's body. Each word wormed into him, telling him yes, it had happened just so. It was there. Fuzzy, unreal, but suddenly so clear in his mind. He'd pulled Fin in. He'd remembered the romances Felicity had given him and wanted to do more than hidden kisses when no one was there. They'd clumsily fallen into his room, like an awkward dance. His bed had been soft as he pulled Fin on top of him. His robe easily undone. Kisses warm as they'd fluttered along his neck and then across his exposed stomach.

Morgan's face felt like it was on fire. He wanted to jump back into the sea, just to cool off again, but instead, he pulled the hood further down to hide how red he must have been.

"Oh." Morgan swallowed. "I see now."

"Yeah," Fin said sadly. "I guess Augustus needed to talk to you. We didn't hear him coming. Didn't even realize the door had opened until he dragged me off you." He shook his head. "I got fired, reamed for being inappropriate with the body of the Divine. I screwed it all up."

"No," Morgan said and Fin finally looked at him again. His eyes were glistening with tears. "No. Allowing me to be human was *not* inappropriate. My body is *not* holy."

Fin scrunched up tighter. "Why didn't you remember? I mean, I know your memories are hazy, but, it's... scary." His gaze grew distant. "When your face lit up seeing Felicity—even just hearing her name—I have to admit I was hurt. I just couldn't understand why you remembered her so well and not me. I've never heard about Divines forgetting a whole person. Especially when you remember it so well now."

Nausea flooded over Morgan. He remembered yelling. He remembered crying. His wrist tight in someone's hand. And then his mouth forced open as something scalding washed down his throat. So much of it, he'd been sick the entire day after. He'd been so quick to attribute the images to a stray soul he'd sent, but maybe those memories were *his.*

And he would never have known if Eryn hadn't said anything. The memories would have stayed ghosts on the edge of all the others.

"T-The Head Prior must have given me too much milk tea," Morgan whispered and Fin raised his eyebrows, confused. "It makes troubling memories less real. Helps me forget it when I'm finished. Sometimes, it just pushes it below all the others so effectively, I no longer remember it beyond a fleeting glimpse." Tears prickled the corner of Morgan's eyes and he dipped his head to blink them back. "They forced me to forget you."

Silence hung between them. Morgan had hated being Divine long before Fin, but the complete loss of part of himself had only made everything worse. He'd known something so uniquely human only to have it stripped away, leaving him alone and estranged from the world. And no one in the priory cared. They'd let it happen. And they'd probably let it happen again if he returned, taking away every single memory. Whatever Joseph promised wouldn't matter; the Head Prior would make it so. He wanted complete control and he'd do anything to have it back.

"I'm sorry," Fin whispered, his voice bridging Morgan back to him. "I'm so sorry." It was as strained as Morgan's had been. "I should have realized. I thought maybe it was better you didn't know me, so I never thought to try and see you. W-When you looked at me, not even knowing *who* I was when I fell on you? I thought, maybe you didn't *want* to remember me. I'd wanted to preserve some sense of normalcy between us." He squeezed his eyes shut and ran his hands through his hair. "I thought you meant to forget. I thought I'd screwed up that badly and it was your choice."

"Did your grandmother know?" Morgan asked.

Fin dropped his gaze. "I didn't tell her what we did. She was so devout. She probably wouldn't have known what to do, but I think she knew anyway. Her last words said as much."

That she was proud of him, no matter what he'd done.

"She must have pieced it together—she knew I liked guys and had no reason to want to join the priory other than the Divine was my age." Fin closed his eyes. "I thought I'd screwed up everything for you when I finally dragged myself home. She let me cry it all out without asking why." He opened his eyes and met Morgan's again. "I should have just told you when you asked me why I'd left the first time. I just froze up. Not knowing what to say or how. I didn't want to hurt you again."

Morgan gently placed his hand over Fin's. It was warm. Fin turned it and gently wrapped his fingers around Morgan's. "You never did," Morgan said. "You made me feel human."

"I'm glad I did." Fin squeezed Morgan's hand gently. "When I started, you were so sad. No one told me why, just that it was how you were. I didn't believe them. All I wanted to do was make you smile. And then slowly, I got to know you—the real you. I didn't mean for it to go any farther than that, but I really liked kissing you. It was worth getting fired, just to see you genuinely smile."

And he had. Over and over again. Even now. Everything they'd done together had a way of worming a smile back on Morgan's lips. Evidence of someone who actually cared about him for him, not for the divinity he could grant.

The sun was dipping into the ocean, lighting Fin's features in gold, and Fin kept hold of Morgan's gaze. He appeared exactly as he had in the fuzzy depth of memory. Everything Morgan wanted in the here and now. His body buzzed, a decision made in the back of his thoughts, and he pressed his lips against Fin's. No veil, no Divine, nothing between them but themselves.

It connected Morgan to all the hazy kisses buried against his will. Reminded him how he'd felt back then. The overwhelming warmth of suddenly being wanted and himself; not a ghost struggling to remember his own self.

Before Morgan lost himself entirely to the warmth of Fin's lips, he drew back and smirked at him. "This time," he said, finding his voice a little breathless as his heart raced, "you can't be fired." Fin's grin turned eager and he leaned back in, cupping the side of Morgan's face.

Someone cleared their throat. Morgan jolted back, practically jumping out of his skin, and Fin whipped around to look beside them.

One of the girls who had been with Eryn stood there; blonde hair crowned her head in a braid and she wore a pink swimsuit with yellow bows practically everywhere.

"Sorry." She made an awkward face, like she definitely hadn't intended to interrupt. "My dad needs help pulling some firewood together. They're gonna light the bonfire soon." She faced Morgan, sizing him up, and decided against it and eyed Fin expectantly instead. "Miss Eryn said one of you could help."

Morgan and Fin peered around the girl, looking for Eryn, and she was still at the shore, face in her palm. At least the interruption hadn't been intentional, but it was pretty funny the more Morgan thought about it, and he had to stifle a snicker.

"I'll help," Fin said after an exaggerated sigh. He kissed Morgan on the cheek before he stood. At least he wasn't running away out of sheer nerves this time. The girl rolled her eyes and took his hand when he was done. She waved at her dad near the woodpile before she dragged over him by the arm.

Other groups had moved closer to the bonfire, laying down their towels and blankets to get a front row seat. Morgan could too. He'd stood and bent over to gather the blanket and their things when he heard Eryn weakly laughing beside him. She'd returned, no children trailing after her, and looked apologetic.

"Sorry about that!" She bent down and secured Fin's camera in his bag before collecting everything else. "I didn't think you'd kiss." She grinned teasingly at Morgan and nudged him in the side. He nudged her right back. "You were looking pissed for a bit there after you *finally* got time together, I thought the girl could diffuse it. And then you were kissing. Everything good, then?"

Morgan returned her smile. "I think so. Thank you for telling me about Fin." He slid his photos into the bag and gently folded his shells into the blanket to pick them up. "It means a lot to me."

"I sort of wished you could have done that at the fair," Eryn said. "A kiss would have been *so* romantic all up in the air."

"Then you would have missed going up," Morgan said. "Having more time to think helped."

She rolled her eyes and drew him into a one-armed hug. She squeezed, smelling of the salt and the sea so close, and only released him after he began to wiggle for freedom. She giggled, grinning at him, and he couldn't help but return it.

"I spy a good spot to set down over there." She bent to grab their cooler. "Bet I can even grab some of whatever it is I'm smelling." She sniffed the air and Morgan followed suit. It made his stomach rumble. "It'll be a *real* meal—much better than all that sugar and our soggy sandwiches!" She shook the cooler as she spoke and laughed. "Come on."

She took the lead, waving at someone nearby, and as Morgan stepped after her, the world shifted beneath his feet. Like it wanted to remind him this was not his world. The sudden jolt of panic made everyone around him still, ghostly apparitions in their place like a nightmare, and a shiver ran down his back. The awful sensation reminding him this would end and he'd forget it all no matter what he did or learned tonight. It rooted itself deep in his thoughts so quickly, digging down into his heart, and squeezed the air out of his lungs.

Fire sparked across the sand, tracing up his legs until it coated his arms, his entire body. His breathing struggled to matter as memories threatened to pull him under. The tea washed down his throat again, scalding. Every single time just to undo anything he'd achieved to keep him controlled. It was wrong. It wasn't real. A daydream of his own making because he expected it whole-heartedly as soon as he returned to the priory.

They'd take it all away, just like Fin. No matter what anyone did.

A hand suddenly looped his wrist, making him jump. The little girl with the sunflower was there again. Except, no—she wasn't. She had already passed through the veil. Morgan forced himself to blink again and finally, the world continued around him. It was a girl, but the one with the yellow bows. She watched him, worried. Eryn had stopped in a conversation with an older woman—maybe the girl's mother.

"Are you okay?" the girl whispered, tilting her head. "You went pale. Mom says when you're suddenly pale, you might throw up. Do you need me to hold your hair?"

Morgan swallowed. "I'm okay," he said. "W-weren't you with Fin?" Her hand was grounding, like he'd drift away otherwise.

The girl shrugged and sidestepped, gently bringing Morgan with her. Aurora and Vesper swept by, arm in arm, making Morgan's skin prickle, but they didn't acknowledge him.

"My arms are puny," the girl said. "Daddy didn't want me to get any splinters." She eyed the shells peeking out of the blanket balanced in Morgan's arm. A warm grin overtook her lips. "Did you like the shells?"

Oh. She'd been one of the ones handing them over. "I do," Morgan said. "Thank you."

The girl nodded, triumphant. "If you ask nicely, I bet my mom can make you a necklace like mine." She looped a finger under the string around her neck and tugged. It held a small shell reflecting a rainbow in the evening sun. "I found this one last year."

Morgan nodded. "Maybe I will."

It wasn't long afterward before the bonfire was finally lit. Morgan wasn't quite sure how he'd take it, but sitting on the blanket with Fin and Eryn beside him filled him with a sense of ease as the branches, logs, and twigs lit up in gold. The whole scene was soothing, the act of burning away something old to leave room for something new. The fire released glowing embers into the darkening sky, each one bright and poignant. It smelled wonderful too, mixed with everything else around them, and not the charred skin and whatever else was trapped in his memories.

Their new spot was up the hill for privacy, but it had a completely unobstructed view of the bonfire. The fair glistened bright in the distance, the lights along the giant wheel glimmering like a constellation. The sound of festivities carried with the wind, adding to the noise already on the beach in a kind of melody of summer's end.

As promised, Eryn scrounged up some *real* food. Morgan got a hamburger with practically everything on it (Eryn admitted the woman working the grill had taken one look at him and slopped it all on, insisting he needed all the extra he could get) and grilled vegetables on the side. Eryn had a smaller hamburger and some kind of creamy salad beside it she ate with gusto. Fin had opted for two burgers himself—simplicity was best, according to him. Eryn made sure Fin took a photo of the food; there wasn't a way to capture the taste, but maybe just looking at it would bring the memory back.

No one minded sharing because many of them recognized Fin and Eryn from previous years. Many of them even paid their condolences to Fin about his grandmother. Maybe because of that alone, the beach maintained its intimacy even as everyone crowded around the bonfire to watch it burn.

Sitting there, watching the flames dance, reminded Morgan of the simplicity of the world. Nothing else really mattered in the end, just what he had in the present. Maybe that'd be enough.

Eventually, once they'd eaten and disposed of their plates, the children returned, their bellies full of their own food, renewing their energy. They wanted to look for glowing shells along the shore since it was dark now, but their parents wouldn't let them unless Eryn agreed to come with. She relented, sighing heavily for show, but was grinning when she stood and Morgan doubted she minded at all.

Morgan nestled himself into Fin and they watched Eryn. Her exaggerated movements while the kids reciprocated and the way they laughed so loud, echoing up and down the shore, kept him at ease. Fin rested his head against Morgan's, drawing his attention.

"Did you..." His voice was sad, slow. Morgan's stomach twisted. He already knew what the question was. "Did you want to go back to the priory after all this?"

It made sense why he'd ask; whether Morgan went or not affected everything Fin might do. He was as much on a precipice of change as Eryn was. If he returned, Morgan's life went back to its damning normalcy and Fin would have to move on alone. Morgan would simply wait for things to change and lose himself bit by bit. Not to mention what the Head Prior would do once he returned a little more lived than before. Photos might not even matter, nor would anything Joseph or Harmony did.

If he stayed, however, he had no one else but Fin. Housing a runaway Divine wouldn't be easy. Hair that wouldn't dye and eyes forever a brilliant shade of gold gave him away to anyone who'd look closely. They might not even be able to stay in Blackburn. Beyond that, Morgan had no real lived experiences and he'd have to rely on Fin entirely until he got a handle on being a normal person. It was so much to ask for in one person alone.

And yet, going back to the priory was death. A reminder of his mortality. One he had been fully willing to throw away until Fin fell into his room. The tomb of the priory really hadn't bothered him before, but now it'd be too stark to ignore. How silent it'd be. How rote the day-to-day would be. How cold everything would be and always had been now that he'd lived with actual warmth.

And yet even still, if he didn't return, who would take his place? Would the Lord of Night simply take another child and have them act in Morgan's place? When a Divine was chosen, the magic let go of any other potentials, so anyone who had been the same as Morgan wouldn't be able to take his place now. His own potential replacements must have been born already, touched the same as Morgan had been by the Lord of Night when he was born. They'd be no more than five years old. Perhaps Marcella would come by more frequently instead, stretching herself thin just to make up for Morgan's absence.

He couldn't do that to anyone.

The question hung in the air. Morgan wasn't able to answer; all he wanted to do was focus on how warm Fin's body was against his. The glow from the bonfire and the way the embers floated into the sky like rising stars. The soft sounds of the waves pushing and pulling the shore. Forget everything else.

"Hey!"

Aurora's voice sang through his thoughts and Morgan stilled. She'd picked her way toward them, sheer shawl back around her shoulders, and the bonfire haloed her in light. She smiled apologetically at them.

"I lost my wedding ring when I was swimming earlier." She showed them her bare ring finger and then nodded toward Eryn and the children at the shore. They were bent over, like they were searching for it. "It's almost too dark to see and I haven't found it yet. Vesper's checking the way back to our bike. Eryn said you could help." She pressed her hands together. "Everyone else is too absorbed in the bonfire. Please?"

Fin leaned away from Morgan and nodded. "I'll help," he said. Aurora beamed at him and left to accost another group nearby glancing in her direction.

Once she'd turned away, Fin bent closer again. "Morgan," he said and gently cupped Morgan's face. "If you need me to take you back, I will. And if not, you can stay with me—I'll make it work. Whatever you decide, just remember: it's all right to be selfish. You are human. I'll love you no matter what." He softly kissed him before he rose and headed after Aurora.

Morgan watched them go, thoughts growing distant as he turned the words over in his head, until he noticed a shadow beside him.

"To be selfish, huh?"

He jumped and looked. Vesper stood there, watching Aurora go with Fin and the others trailing after her. The fire glinted off his white hair and lit the bright gray of his eyes. Immediately, Morgan went to ask why he was there and not doing what Aurora had said, but then he sat beside Morgan and gently touched his hand.

The entire world shifted upon the touch and a ghostly breath blew between them, like the very veil was opening up.

Because it wasn't Vesper beside him; it was the Lord of Night.

XIV.
WHEN THE VEIL IS THIN

Everything slowed and quieted, but it wasn't Morgan's panic making it so. It was truly like he and the Lord of Night were the only two who existed. The waves had grown still, Eryn and Fin and everyone else had ceased to move, and everything had taken a spectral hue as it grew dark and dim. Except for Aurora. Because she wasn't really Aurora, Morgan now realized. A golden halo crowned her honey brown hair, denoting her as the Lady of Dawn.

The Lord of Night hadn't taken his gaze off Morgan. The deep black pools of his eyes reflected the stars he'd scattered across the night sky. His hair was the stark snow-white locks reminiscent of a Divine's and it had grown from what it had been as

Vesper's; it crowned his head as wisps and came down longer on one side, carefully swept over his shoulder. He didn't wear his celestial vestments, instead merely his shroud of stars across his shoulders, covering Vesper's white tank, motorcycle jeans, and the bright red bracelet around one wrist. The outfit felt so mundane and wrong on the very celestial being responsible for death.

The thump of Morgan's heart and his panicked breathing were the only sounds in the stillness. The Lord of Night made none; he simply stared. Waited. He'd followed Morgan all the way from the priory. All those glimpses hadn't been chance; he'd been there the entire time. Morgan had screwed up *so* much, the Lord of Night finally eschewed tradition and appeared before him in truth.

"I'm not trying to scare you," the Lord of Night finally said, his voice the soft rumble Morgan remembered hiding behind his own during a sending.

"Oh." A nervous titter escaped Morgan's throat as he raised his eyebrows. "This—*this* isn't trying to scare me?" The words left his mouth with anger surging behind them and he jerked his arm toward the frozen world around them. "You specifically made it so I was alone to take me here. This is what you've been trying to do since you found us. You—"

The Lord of Night frowned and Morgan bit his

lip to keep from continuing. "I needed to speak with you alone." The Lord flicked a glance at Fin and Eryn. "They've made it *incredibly* difficult. Always looking after you, even when they were far. I thought we'd be having this conversation at the motel, but you left the room and Aurora was not able to truly grasp your friend's entire attention. Then I was tied up with Prior Augustus as you hid in the trees. And then, when your friends were changing, that boy *knew* you were nervous and I couldn't risk him coming out to witness this. Humans I have not touched aren't meant to." His features shifted, some humanity blooming into him once more, and the black in his eyes receded into the soft gray Vesper's had been. Morgan blinked; Vesper had returned altogether. "Would Vesper's guise help? I mean not to frighten you, Morgan, but I need you here with me."

Vesper was better than the Lord of Night. Human, somehow, even if Morgan knew better now. Morgan nodded and dropped his hands into his lap, attempting to piece his thoughts back together. He didn't want to be angry. It'd do him no good.

"You followed us," Morgan said.

"I did." Vesper nodded. "But know I am not following you on *their* whim." Not that Morgan thought he was; no clergy could control the whim of a celestial being no matter how full of themselves they were. "I was... curious as to why you left the priory and have come this far from it."

His curiosity, his lack of understanding, sent fire throughout Morgan's chest. He wanted to scream—how could he not understand? How could he not plainly see everything Morgan had been going through? He bit the scream back all the same. He had to be calm. Rational.

"Curious?" Morgan repeated. "You made me—a *child*—Divine." He stressed the words, trying not to let them shake, even as his entire body did. "You never let me live. What did you think I was going to do if given the chance?"

Part of him was terrified of how his words sounded. The anger was too clear. The condemnation too strong. One didn't just blame a celestial being right to his face that it was his fault, no matter how true it was. Yet, Morgan had done it, the words right on his tongue. To his credit, Vesper didn't flinch. His expression remained morose and concerned, not at all shocked.

"I am not here to lecture you," he said. "I am trying to understand."

"How can you?" Morgan moved away from him, intending to stand, but just as his hand left the blanket, it folded into the world. He would have fallen after it, but the Lord of Night—not Vesper—reached forward and jerked Morgan back onto the blanket. As soon as he'd settled back down, Vesper's face had returned.

"W-What was that?" Morgan asked as Vesper released him.

"You are in the veil on a solid square I made for us to speak privately. Its edge is the same as the blanket." Vesper drew his hand in front of himself. The air shimmered in its wake. "The veil is enormously vast, passing through the world like water and is not a solid plane. Please stay here with me. If you fall, even I may not be able to retrieve you."

No moving away, then. Morgan gingerly readjusted his legs, making sure he was as solidly on the blanket as he could be, and in his silence, Vesper had gazed outward at the bonfire. The flames were still golden in the veil and the firelight twinkled in Vesper's eyes, reflecting the real world.

Morgan didn't know what to say and stayed silent. The god wanted to speak to *him*; not the other way around. Waiting was no better. Nerves made Morgan tremble, a million different scenarios of what would happen flying through his thoughts. None of them good.

Vesper turned his attention to the tote bags and

reached into the one Morgan had put the photos in. Morgan jerked to stop him, but quickly retrieved his hand as all Vesper did was examine them, one by one. Soon, a small smile came to his lips.

"You've had quite the two days," he said.

"Don't hurt them," Morgan said, aware of how small his voice sounded.

The look Vesper gave him oscillated between the human and the Lord of Night. Both hurt. He slid them back into the bag, safely nestled with everything else, and faced Morgan fully.

"I would never. They are precious memories."

Silence moved between them once more, just as terse as it had been before. Finally, Vesper cut his gaze downward, looking at his hands, and furrowed his brow. "I will admit, you were extraordinarily young when I touched you as Divine. I cannot dispute it. Nor can I dispute that perhaps, the clergy was hasty in their treatment of you. A mound of mistakes unraveling finally to this."

The assessment was clinical and cold. Bereft of any emotion related to guilt. It furthered Morgan's anger. All he wanted to do was throw himself at the Lord of Night, shake him, punch him, do something to show what his words were failing to convey. Instead, he breathed out sharply through his nose.

"Why didn't you stop them?"

Vesper considered him sadly. "I vowed not to interfere."

The Lord and Lady made the world, they breathed life into its people, and led them through to their final resting places until the cycle began anew. Except, as Fin's words echoed in Morgan's thoughts, they had their hands in *everything* therein. Vowing not to interfere didn't mean anything when they did so brazenly.

Morgan threw his arm out toward the beach. "And this isn't interfering?" he asked. "You being Vesper isn't? Is he even real?"

"I am him, but he is not me," Vesper said, the cadence of the Lord of Night's voice poignant behind his own. "He is one of many physical bodies that allow me through the veil in truth on such days. Otherwise, I cannot. I am not physical."

Morgan dropped his arm. "If you can do this and *party*"—a flicker of annoyance passed Vesper's face, betraying the celestial being within—"then you can do your own goddamn job." The words were wracked with a sob Morgan hadn't known was even there.

Vesper sighed and held out his hand for Morgan, waiting. The skin glistened with starlight just below the surface, following his veins. Slowly, Morgan took the hand, or at least, he felt like he did. There was something off about it that wasn't there when he touched Morgan before. Now, the hand hardly felt like it was real, as though his thoughts simply tricked him into believing it so.

"As it is," Vesper said, the unearthly tenor of the Lord of Night fully settling in his voice, "the veil is thin on days like today. Equinoxes and solstices, and the days leading up to and leading away." He let Morgan go, his hand completely sliding through Morgan's fingers. "The Lady and I can transcend physically into the mortal world on days like today. It allows us to see what the world has cultivated in truth, not through the facsimile of memories filtered through the veil."

No. He was lying. It was a bold lie and an excuse. Countless equinoxes and solstices have gone by and Morgan had remained alone.

Morgan brought his knees to his chest, glancing away. The conversation wasn't going anywhere. His heart still hadn't calmed down. "What do you want from me?" he whispered.

"To talk to you," Vesper stressed and though Morgan expected annoyance—they both *knew* why he was here—Vesper's voice had grown desperate. Even without looking, Morgan felt the Lord of Night's gaze settle on him. "I missed my chance to talk to Divine Lilia and I *should* have spoken to her."

No one had told Morgan why Lilia had passed. Morgan had been present for her sending as Marcella had used her to show him how, but she'd refused to allow Morgan to handle Lilia's soul himself. Morgan only learned later it was customary for the Divine taking the place of another to personally send their soul as the previous Divine's memories would help with teaching, but Marcella had been so adamant on not letting Morgan touch it. At twelve, he hadn't minded.

During the sending, Marcella had filled the silence that night with what she knew of Lilia. Superficial details Morgan hardly recalled now. The clergy in the priory hardly spoke her name, like it was bad luck, and Morgan assumed it was what happened to previous Divines. They became ghosts. Gone. Simply a tool to be used. Morgan had already become his own ghost, after all. It had made sense at the time. Only Joseph had spoken about her fondly, but it'd been such a short remembrance.

He lifted his head and studied Vesper. "What happened to Lilia? No one's told me."

Vesper was quiet a long time. He fiddled with the red cord adorning his wrist, gaze very distant and very sad. When he spoke, it was with the Lord of Night's clear voice, not his own. "She was vastly unhappy," he said. "The clergy didn't see it, at least, didn't claim to see it or ignored it altogether. She did her job; they had no interest in her mental state otherwise." His frown deepened. "Even I did not quite parse it until it was too late. She didn't fully divulge her feelings and no one listened to what were clear cries for help they see now." He matched Morgan's gaze, his eyes clear of flickering flames. "I held fast to my rule and she took her own life."

Silence pushed between them. Morgan should have realized it, given the way she'd become the un-person. The way Marcella had spoken so sadly about her; not just because a friend was dead, but because she'd missed the cries herself.

"And," Vesper continued, "before she died, while on her excursions from the priory during solitude, she poisoned the potential Divines in Blackburn, essentially taking them with her." Morgan went cold. "It was her way of getting back at me. Curiously, she missed you by pure chance. I had no choice."

The anger snapped back. "No," Morgan shouted. "You *had* a choice! You didn't have to pick a literal child! You could have done something else!"

Another sigh left Vesper's throat. Human, frustrated, everything a celestial being wasn't. "I did not want this for you, Morgan. Even I see how hard it is for someone so young to give up a life they'd hardly even lived. However, there was no one else. I could not take from Marcella's potentials; they knew nothing of Blackburn and would not have made the connection needed."

Morgan opened his mouth to argue, but Vesper held up his hand. Morgan intended to speak despite the motion, but found his voice stolen away. He pressed his hands to his throat, eyes wide.

"Please. I am speaking."

The Lord of Night's guise shuddered into focus, stealing Vesper completely away. His entire splendor came through this time, his celestial vestments mirroring a Divine's own, only black and gold with a vibrant red sash, and his shroud of stars was fastened around his shoulders, spilling across him as an entire cosmos. With his real self in such stark focus, so too came the knowledge death was imminent, but his face remained soft, kind, and most of all: worried.

"I have guided your hands. I have whispered to you as you've grown," the Lord of Night continued, "and still, it's led to this. The clergy wanted someone absent of feeling, of any true memory, so they could avoid another Lilia, but it's left you open to internalize memories you couldn't fully send. It wasn't supposed to be this way. You were never supposed to be the Divine they locked in a tower until they needed you."

The fire that flickered at the edge of his dreams.

A memory not his own simply becoming his because it was so real and stark, having no home of its own other than Morgan. Maybe in the beginning, the Head Prior sought to protect him, but he'd gone too far. Whatever the Head Prior's intentions, it didn't erase his own failings, especially when his own desire was for complete control over Morgan.

"Let me live," Morgan whispered, testing his voice when the Lord of Night didn't continue. When it worked, Morgan raised it. "Let me have true memories. Let me leave the divinity behind."

"It's not easy breaking a promise you made to the world."

"You already have." Tears slipped unbidden down Morgan's cheeks. He released the tension in his shoulders and took the Lord of Night's hands in his own. "You plan to take me back, don't you?"

The Lord of Night gently turned his hands to wrap his fingers around Morgan's. This time, the hand felt more solid. "It's your choice," he said, slowly rounding the syllables. "Not mine. The role of Divine is sacred. It's meant to help us continue this world. I need Divines to help souls through—they are lost, broken, and trapped otherwise despite my intentions." He studied Morgan's arms. The bruises were harsh in the veil as crisscrossing blue and purple lines. The Lord of Night gently ran a finger across one. "Birth has not this issue; souls want to be replanted and reborn." His face tightened. "Your role was never meant to be something you dreaded. Not something that erased who you are. You were never supposed to be punished for not being proper enough in their eyes."

There was righteous anger echoing in the Lord's voice, but it didn't matter to Morgan. "You let them do it," he said.

"I am not to interfere. Their judgement *will* come."

Morgan bit his lip, trying to remind himself of reality. "You're not to interfere and-and that lets people die scared and alone. You know people die without Divines. Like in that field."

The Lord of Night's inaction. His refusal to open the veil himself and guide souls under his own power.

"You say you won't interfere," Morgan continued, "but you were there with me when I sent the little girl." He held the Lord's hand tighter. "You pulled me out of their grasp in my dream. You are already interfering; you can't just pick and choose what counts or not." More tears slid down his cheeks. "Please, interfere and let me be Morgan. Not the Divine. I want *my* life back."

The Lord of Night watched him for a moment

before facing the fire. It was moving in the veil, even though everything else remained still. "I know," he whispered. The fire leapt up, sending embers into the flickering stars.

Morgan released the Lord's hands and drew Fin's jacket tightly around himself. Even it had ceased to give him any warmth here. There was more to be said, Morgan was sure, but everything else left him too numb. Except one thing. "You've followed me from the priory, haven't you?" He glanced at the Lord of Night who gave him a slight nod. "All because..."

"I heard you. What would I say if you entered my graces too early?" The Lord tilted his head, like he meant to find Morgan's gaze when he looked away. "I grew worried, and as it happens, the veil is thin on days like today." He stood and his robes of starlight swished around him with the movement. They dragged behind him as he sat beside Morgan, bringing with him warmth reminiscent of a crackling fire.

"And I know," he continued, "if I force you to return, you *will* come to me too early." He reached up and gently pushed Morgan's hood down. "I am not heartless."

Time was thawing around them as the veil receded. The Lord must have said what he'd wanted to and slowly let the world return. The fire crackled, audible, and the waves crashed on the shore once more, reflecting the glimmer of the bonfire. Voices echoed across the shore from faraway, even as everyone remained still.

"The choice is yours. You are allowed to be selfish."

Morgan's heart lurched at the words, even more tears trying to spring forth, and he squeezed his eyes shut, tightening his shoulders. "No," he said, sudden second thoughts taking hold. "I'll be dooming souls. Dooming another literal child. Making it so much harder for Marcella."

He could hardly stand being Divine, but he didn't know if he could stand being Morgan if it meant he was damning another child to go through what he did. More tears silently followed the others down his cheeks and continued unabated until the Lord of Night gently wiped them. He didn't remove his hand from Morgan's face right away and instead, traced it down to Morgan's chin before he gently took it. Morgan didn't resist as the Lord of Night tilted Morgan's head to look at him.

"Perhaps," he murmured, "I can be asked to break one promise with another."

"What?" Morgan blinked. "W-What happens if you do?"

Vesper returned in his entirety, the vestments of starlight gone and the only clue he was the Lord at all was the red cord around his wrist again. "I don't know," he said. "Not until I walk the realm as Vesper in truth. Not as a simulacrum of humanity."

"But what about souls waiting for you so they can cross?" Morgan whispered.

"I am a god. I am everywhere," Vesper said, tilting his head. "Although, I truly cannot say what will happen. It's something I've never done, but you needn't worry. It is not your burden."

Somehow, the idea unnerved Morgan even more than discarding his divinity did. It felt wrong to ask a celestial being to walk the world as a human, just so Morgan could live the life he wanted. It was blasphemous. Selfish. Yet, it was everything he wanted.

He swallowed, choosing his words carefully. "But what right do I have to be selfish?"

"Every," Vesper replied. "Are you telling me no?" He smirked, raising an eyebrow, and Morgan mouthed a million responses, not a single one voicing itself. "The Lady granted you this life. I cannot take it and force you to do anything." He gently ran his fingers through Morgan's hair. The air followed, trickling across Morgan's scalp like a ghost.

"I have given you your black hair once more,"

Vesper whispered, the white in his own growing vibrant as it ate away the black roots. He leaned forward and kissed Morgan on one eye, and then the next. When Vesper retreated, his own eyes flickered gold like fire. "And my gray eyes." He leaned back, taking Morgan's chin in hand, and ran a thumb across Morgan's lips. He shook his head. "Your friend seems rather fond of your teeth, perhaps I should leave those?" He smiled, a little wider than before, and Morgan sighted the sharp teeth within.

Morgan covered his mouth, snapping back, his cheeks hot. Around him, the world was more and more real. People moved, the chatter became more than an echo, and the fire even brighter as someone fed a bundle of sticks into it to keep it alive.

"I cannot take the Divine magic from you," Vesper continued. "That was my holy gift. I would never take it back. Should you hear a soul wanting, the desire to send it will remain. It's up to you whether you do or don't." He tucked a lock of Morgan's hair behind his ear. "However, should you cross the threshold in the Blackburn Priory, all divinity will return and Vesper will cease to be.

"Take this night to be Morgan in truth before you make your decision." Vesper retrieved his hand. "Should you change your mind, simply return. Meanwhile, Vesper as myself shall act in your stead.

I *will* make the clergy understand." He smiled gently. "If after you've lived your life and wish to take the mantle again, I will happily return it." He leaned in and pressed their foreheads together.

All at once, Vesper's face shifted back into the Lord of Night's. "And, should I never see you again until you grace my halls, consider it a well-lived life. Do not regret your decision, whatever it may be." He pressed his lips to Morgan's forehead and stood, Vesper's guise hiding the celestial being within.

The veil departed entirely, leaving Morgan starkly in reality, and it felt too real. The fire was so bright against the clear night sky, so golden and warm. The waves smoothed across the shore, the sound so close. A litany of cheers rang out, drowning out the waves, and Morgan turned toward them. Her arm outstretched, Aurora displayed the ring now upon her finger and it gleamed against the firelight. Eryn and Fin stood beside her with the small gathering she had enlisted to help. She was beaming as she turned and waved at Vesper coming down for her. He wrapped her up in a tight embrace, lifting her off the ground.

Fin and Eryn were the only ones who really looked at Vesper and startled; they must have seen the glimmer of golden eyes—Morgan's eyes. His pure white hair—Morgan's hair. The children simply didn't care; without a distraction, they were pulling at Eryn's arms, cheering about marshmallows, and before they dragged her away, she eyed Fin and nodded toward Morgan.

Fin turned and his jaw dropped. Morgan numbly felt his hair. It really must have been black. *His* hair. Not the Divine's. Tears went down his cheeks again, warm against his cold skin. He barely registered time moving by before Fin dropped to his knees in front of him, out of breath from running back.

"It's black," Fin whispered as he slid his fingers through Morgan's hair. He balked when he noticed Morgan's eyes. "W-What happened?"

Tears bubbled up again and Morgan didn't want them to fall. He didn't want to cry over something he'd desperately wanted. He wrapped his arms around Fin and pulled him into the blanket. They landed with a thump and Morgan held Fin as tight as he could. The tears came anyway, happy, but sad at the same time as Morgan buried his face into Fin's shoulder. Fin had gone still, but soon relaxed and whispered soothing words that it would be all right into Morgan's hair. Morgan managed to calm himself down soon enough so he could at least look at Fin properly.

"I-I love you too," Morgan said, his heart still

thumping too hard in his chest. "F-For everything you've done for me—even when I didn't remember you. If-If not for you, I-I—"

Fin took Morgan's face gently in his hands and held it. "I know," he said and wiped the stray tears with his thumb. "I know. You don't have to say so." Once more, Fin drew his fingers through Morgan's hair, brushing it back. "What even *was* he? What'd he do?"

"He was never Vesper," Morgan said, trying so hard not to trip over his words. "And I'm fine—he was the Lord of Night—he let me go." Fin gave him a confused look and Morgan brought them both back up to a sitting position. He flashed Fin a wide grin, showing off all his teeth. "And I still have my sharp teeth."

It made Fin laugh, like it was the most absurd thing in the world, and he pressed his forehead against Morgan's as he tried to stifle it. Morgan started laughing too and before long, they fell back into the blanket within each other's arms like nothing else mattered. Morgan didn't mind, especially as once the laughter tapered off, Fin drew him into a deep kiss and held him there until they were both breathless. Once they parted, Fin had a satisfied grin on his lips, and put an arm around Morgan's back to press him closer as they gazed at the sky together.

Fireworks flashed in the sky, shooting high above the beach, and elicited oohs and ahhs all around them. Colors glimmered across everything, reflected off the waves themselves, and cast multi-color glows as more and more fireworks lifted into the sky.

"Can we stay here?" Morgan whispered, resting his head against Fin. "Just like this? Watch the stars and the colors and not get up until dawn?"

Fin paused, eyebrows high as he searched Morgan's expression, but the hesitation melted before long. He kissed Morgan's cheek. "All night. I promise."

They took one more photo together, the last one Fin had in the camera, and Morgan made sure to smile like he meant it. The photo came out crooked and dark, but as Morgan gazed at himself—his black hair, his gray eyes, the still awkward smile showing sharp teeth—it truly felt like it was him.

As he memorized how he and Fin looked to-gether in a single captured moment, he didn't realize Fin was peppering kisses along his jaw until he turned and they kissed properly again. They parted breathless a second time and packed up the camera with all the photos so they could lie back and watch the stars. More and more colors had sprayed themselves across the sky, lighting up the beach in a grand finale all at once, and the lingering embers became fleeting stars in their own right.

The night crawled on by and Morgan wanted to be nowhere else. The bonfire eventually dulled to a gentle glow kept alive by other stargazers and by then, Eryn had returned with no children in tow. She smiled at their pile on the blanket and Fin beckoned her down while Morgan grinned expectantly at her. She blew out a teasing sigh before she drew a second blanket free and curled up with them. It was Morgan's blanket, all the colors in the world in vibrant, variegated strands, and she laid it across the three of them as she nestled in on Fin's other side.

A motorcycle roared late into the night, but even as Morgan craned his neck to peer up the incline, he couldn't see Vesper or Aurora before it left. The sound soon echoed in such a way, it made shivers wash down Morgan's back, reminding him of the veil.

Morgan supposed it didn't matter if he saw them or not before they left. In some way, he supposed, the Lord was actually always there, listening. He rested his head against Fin again and breathed him in. He smelled just like Eryn had; the salt and the ocean both. Fin had fallen asleep, as had Eryn, their chests rising and falling with slow, even breaths.

Morgan never wanted to move. Maybe it was imperfect. Maybe it really wouldn't last. Maybe it was truly selfish and something he should never have asked for. But whatever came next was *his* decision. No one else's.

He didn't want to fall asleep. He didn't even want to see dawn, only because then it meant he'd know his own choice as Morgan, not as the Divine. And part of him didn't want to see it and everything that happened afterward.

All he wanted was to live in this single, timeless moment he'd captured for himself. It belonged to him and him alone and he never wanted to let it go.

Acknowledgments

Writing's always been a little solitary for me and though I don't know quite a lot of people yet, there are a handful of people that without their support, this story wouldn't be here today.

First, I have to thank my mom as cliché as it sounds! She's always my first reader no matter what I've written and it means a lot to have her support. Right after my mom is my sister who is often the second person to read my words and always has very thoughtful comments. Rounding out the top three is Miranda, friend for over ten years and always right there to devour whatever I've written. It means more to me than I can parse into words.

So many people read this in its various drafts, back when it was just shy of a novella all the way until it became the novel it is today! Aowna, Brianna, CDcontainer/12-Amu, Kyla, Zachary (Zahn), Desmond, Rob, Justine, R.K. Ashwick, Isy, the Tremendously Awesome Writer's Fabulous Critique Group (gosh that name is long), Monster Manor, and if I have forgotten anyone, please forgive me—my brain is eternally scattered. Although I've endured many rejections, your comments and comradery have made it all the more bearable.

And, of course, I want to thank my readers for taking a chance on this slightly off-beat story that doesn't seem to quite fit anywhere. Thank you very much for reading!

About the Author

S. Jean (she/they) is a queer sci-fi & fantasy author writing whatever strikes their fancy at any given moment. When not writing or dreaming of what to write, they can be found dabbling in game dev and drawing!

For more information, visit: https://sjean.carrd.co/